Pain

....

Jenna Mikkel

Contents

Prologue

Jason I started kissing her jaw but not kissing her lips, I like to tease her

"Jason please... " she moans grabbing my hair. "Patience baby, do you know what I'm gonna do with you?". I keep assaulting her neck by bitting and sucking down her soft skin. In response she just moans and tilt her neck giving me more access.

"You make me so hard when you moan", I started undressing her. "I'm gonna eat your pussy and when I'm done, you would be cumming so hard only with my mouth and my fingers".

Jason Laszlo Knight is 29 years , a Billionaire and CEO of Knight Enterpri ses.Only works hard for his family. Everyone is afraid of him, treats women as objects. He is having a traumatic and painful past and is very reserved. But she changes everything and breaks the wall that he has build for years.

Kira Regina White is 28 years, a surgeon and started practice in CityMed Hospital. Always busy with her work she doesn't live up her life. She helps people to go through their pain and understands them. She doesn't date anyone because of her past relationship.

When they both cross path with each other, will they both be able to take away each others pain? Or will they cause more pain to each other?

Explore the journey filled with joy, drama, pain, tears and love.

Chapter 1- KIRA

K IRA

My day starts with buzzing off my alarm, freshup and have a long hot shower and then have some breakfast and go for a long 10 hour work at CityMed Hospital. No fun, no time for any hangouts with my friends. Same routine everyday, rarely get holiday at weekends... I imagine if this is going to be my life forever....

Their is huge bang on door that got me out of my thoughts, "Are you going to be sleeping in bed for whole day, or get your ass out of bed and get ready for work", April shouted her lungs out, I am sure the neighbours have heard it too.

April is my best friend, supporter and one of the closest persons who knows everything about me. Not only April lives with me but also Maximus and Julius. Yes they both are twins. Maximus is a playboy, who always get laid with every woman he finds attractive, just like he changes his clothes. He rarely lives with us, just hangouts for a movie night, If he is free... As for Julius... He is completely different from Maximus. He is a gay and a sweetheart who is understanding, and ready to help no matter what.

"We can't be late for work again, Dr. Ron will eat up our jobs, and I will not be able to date any hot guys ever", Julius says while having his breakfast.

"It doesn't makes any sense of you dating the guys with our job", April replied while serving food to Maximus.

"Well, most of the men like to date a hot doctor like me", he smirks at April, just to annoy her.

"Please, we have no interest in discussing your personal love life". I roll my eyes and take a seat beside April.

"So, who is your new falvour today", April starts the topic of discussion. "Are you jealous April, because you didn't have a shot with me", replys sending a wink to her.

"Fuck you", she flips him off. We all laugh hard, we have a great time spending with each other.

Being a surgeon it is a difficult job, it often keeps you busy. All four of us worked hard our ass to get in this position. _______________

"Look he is watching you again, I knew he has a crush on you", April said before she made a fist and hit it right on my shoulder. I winced at the contact, it hurt, a lot.

I took a quick peek and watched Lance spy on us from the canteen. When he was caught staring, he quickly walked out from canteen feeling embarrassed.

Lance is cute, respectful and kind guy. He is indeed a women's fantasy.... But not mine. I was expecting something different, something menacing and agony. I know I was thinking out of the box, but I wanted something more, rather then having a boring life.

"When was the last time you had sex?" I look at April in disbelief.

"April, I've been too busy working as surgeon to be having sex." I roll my eyes and check my next shift.

"Kira, you're my best friend. I want you to get laid, have some fun.Take a break." She sighs.

We get a message on our phone, saving me from this awkward situation.

"Quick, Their is an emergency. A young man has met with an accident and is badly injured in ward 15."

Chapter - 2 JASON

J ASON

"Strip"The woman standing in front of me doesn't respond, but gives me a flirty simle. I hate those women, who doesn't follow my orders and I hate saying it twice.

"Strip", this time I said in a harsh tone. I am sure she felt a flutter of trepidation in her stomach causing her shiver sightly. I love to see the kind of effect I have on people.

She is completely naked in front of me. I give her the contract papers, but she signs it without reading it.Bitch, I'm going to teach her a lesson later.

"You signed the contract without even reading it, Anyways.. . . Let me explain the rules for you", I said in a rough and demanding voice.

Rule No. 1- "Whatever is going to happen, stays within this four walls. You won't contact me or meet me after, this is just for one night and make sure you won't show me your fucking face again".

Rule No. 2- "You will obey and follow my orders without any hesitation".

Rule No. 3- "Remember, I am the one who controls everything in here. You won't speak until you're given my permission".

Rule No. 4 - "You will only call me, 'Sir'.

Rule No.5- "The last and most important rule is, You will not touch me."

"I promise to give you the pleasure you devour for, but you will not touch me or any of my body parts".

She had a puzzled look on her face, she opens and close her mouth again trying to question me. I knew what she was imagining in her fucking head.

I break the silence, "Dare to break any of these rules, I will make sure you won't see the sunlight again", saying in menacing and angry tone.

"Understood".

"Y-Y-Yes Sir."

Good to see that she was sacred of me. "Now, be a good little slut and spread your legs for me..."

I can't really call myself a dominant, because I'm not. I usually like people to see in pain and make them suffer, as most of them deserved it and most of them loved to be in pain.

I'm CEO of Knight Enterprises, a Billionaire. My Grandfather has lot of faith in me and he believes that I could handle it perfectly...... And I did. Past few years I worked hard, had many sleepless nights, just to live up for everyone's expectations.

I hate it. People see me as a man who has everything and anything I want. But I don't...... They don't know the demons that are caged inside of me, they don't know how cruel, heartless, lonely and ruthless I am.

So, to release my stress and my demons, I make other people suffer. Whether is it my business work or the sexual life.

After fucking her, I remove the condom and throw it in dustbin.

"Fuck", she grunted.

"You are not even a good fuck, you couldn't even satisfied me bitch. You are just a waste of time", I walked out from bed.

"Collect your clothes, get out NOW!!!". I shouted at her, which made her shiver.

"P-Please just let me s-spend one night here, I t-think I won't be able to w-walk", she said in breathless tone.

"I don't fucking care, just get out or I will throw you out myself."I was raging in anger, as I couldn't deal with this woman anymore and it doesn't matter what will happen to her. I don't even know her name and don't fucking care to even ask her.

"You are a psychopath", she stated while lifting her clothes.

I let it slide, because I was not in my fucking mindset to deal with it. If she stays one more second here,I might kill her by myself.

After working on some files, I decided to take a nap, but my phone rang.... It was my mother, I try to ignore it. But she couldn't stop calling me, so I finally lifted my phone.

"Thank god Jason, you lifted your phone. Arlo has met with an accident, we are on the way to CityMed Hospital. Please arrive fast."

Chapter - 3 Accident

K IRA

"Patient details - Aron KnightMale, 25 year old, had a car accident, has a severe brain injury and lost much of blood."

"Hurry take him to the operating room", Dr. Ron gave us the instructions, as we got ready for the operation.

The patient's condition was worse because the skull has been Violently striked against front and back, his blood vessels are ruptured as it not allowing the blood to collect between the brain and spinal cord.

His condition is getting worse and worse, a single mistake will lead him to prayalasis, vision problems, stiff neck and even worse he can die.

We are now performing Craniontomy treatment. I don't know why their is huge tension among the senior surgeons, as they were whispering something to each other. I am sure they have performed many difficult surgery as compared to this.

After a perid of long 3-4 hours surgery, the patient was out of danger, we all have a relieved simles on our face. Indeed, it was the most difficult surgery of my life and I'm glad, I was part of it.

"What's happening outside, why is it so noisy?". I ask.

"You don't know what's happening?". Liza my colleague was kinda shocked.

"I really have no idea, am I missing out something ?".

"Liza, I will explain her, she is always obsessed with her job, so she doesn't know any gossips." April shrugs.

"Actually, Kira he is _______ She was cut off by Dr. Ron.

"Kira, I need you to assist with me for communicating with patients family". He said in stern voice and doesn't even wait for my answer.

"No wonder he wants you to assist with him, I'm not all good with this stuff. You should probably get going." She gives me a hug and leaves.

I don't know, but I think I can understand people's pain and communicate with them as my own people. So I guess this is the reason why the doctor's appoint me with them.

We came out of the operating room to meet the patient's family. From a short distance, I can see someone quarrel with the nurses. There are quite a few people, assuming the patient is having a big family.

Everyone is rambling and their is overlapping of all the voices in the room, but I hear a strong and husky voice above all. I never thought someone's voice would sound so sexy yet strong.

As I approached slowly to the crowd, suddenly my heart started beating fast. What the fuck is wrong with me. His back was faced to me. By looking at him, I can say he is muscular man with defined muscles. How can someone have such a perfect back?

I was kinda curious to see him, wonder how he looks from front.

"Please be calm sir, other patients are getting disturbed", Dr. Ron complained.

The man turned his back...... Holy Moly mother of Jesus, Fuck....... Indeed he is a gorgeous man,sexy as hell. He has a beautiful face, with ocean eyes and a stubble beard which suites his face.

He is perfect, perfect in every way. He is so attractive and handsome. And his lips...... Never have I ever met a man with such alluring lips as his, I bet it tastes sweet as _______ Fuck, what the hell am I thinking. I don't even know him, still he is having such a effect on me.

Focus Kira, you are here to have a serious conversation, not to drool on a man. Be professional.

"I don't fucking care about the other patients, just tell me what is wrong with my brother? Why is it taking so much time? I demand answers Now!!!".

Wow..... I totally have a crush on him. Yet, I think I saw him before..... But I don't remember it. Focus.

So I speak up, " Sir, I know its a tough time but your brother is out of danger. He is fine and currently stable. We can discuss this further in the office. Just calm down."

His gaze settles down at me. Shit, I feel nervous as he checks me out from top to bottom. Is he checking me out? Then his eyes stops at me. He just stares at me. Do I have something on my face? Is it my make up? But I don't usually wear a lot of make up. Hundreds of questions were popping in my head. Why isn't he saying anything?

"She is right, you need to calm down. Your brother needs you", a middle age woman said to the man. He slightly nods, still keeping his gaze on me.

Dr. White will show the way to the office, please follow her", he said to the family members by showing the direction.

He looks an d me and says, "Take them to the office and discuss the condition, I will control the situation in here and join you later.

Great, fucking great. How am I going to say anything, if he keeps on staring at me.

I nod and show them they way to the office.

"Please take your seats".

"Will you just fucking tell us now", the brute shouted.

Chapter - 4 First Sight

J ASON

"Thank god Jason you lifted your phone, Arlo has met with an accident. We are on the way to CityMed Hospital, please arrive fast."

I'm numb.I try to recall what just she said. She was sacred.

Arlo is my small brother. He adores me, he even says I'm an inspiration to him I don't know why. Whenever I feel low, he is always there to cheer me up. He is mechievous and playful. He is maybe a fully grown up man, but still he has a playful child in himself.

No matter what, my brother is certainly a gift sent from God. Not only him but my whole family. The only one good thing I have with me is my family. After my grandfather, it is my responsibility to protect my family no matter what.

I rushed and call my driver. I call the administrator of the hospital. I certainly give him a warning and tell him to get the best surgeons for my brother. They will surely take it seriously as I pay a huge amount of charity to the hospital and been one of the board members.

I don't know how these people got the information, but the media is crowded outside of the hospital. They just want news to get the trps for their channel. I call more security because I can't trust anyone one, even the hospital staff.

I'm raging in anger, I'm about 10 seconds away from losing it. I try to control my anger, but I can't. He is in the ICU for about more than 3-4 hours, but we don't get any news about him. My mother is shedding tears, my aunt is handling her. My grandfather is terrified and uncle is reassuring him. My cousins are sad and tensed.

I disliked watching them in this condition. Enough...

"What's taking so much time? Where the fuck is my brother", I started yelling at the staff. Maybe I'm a selfish man, but I can't watch my family depressed.

I couldn't help my brother. He is fighting all alone in there. All I can do is to take out my anger on them... And I did. I was alone rambling in the ward. Rest of them tired to calm me, but I couldn't.

Now everyone in the ward started speaking, but out of all, my voice is clearly audible.

"Please be calm sir, other patients are getting disturbed", a voice came from behind. I turn myself around, he is a doctor but I don't care. I demanded answers.

"I don't fucking care about other patients, just tell me what is wrong with my brother? Why is it taking so much time? I demand answers now!!", I yelled in a harsh tone. Their is pin drop silence in the ward.

"Sir, I know it's a tough time but your brother is out of danger and is fine. He is currently stable. We can discuss this futher in the office. Just calm down", a sweet angelic voice came beside me. I never heard such a gentle voice before.

I turn my face and I saw HER.......

I'm shocked. She is...... She is so beautiful. God, I don't think I ever saw someone so attractive as her. I take a moment to admire her beauty, as my eyes scan her from top to bottom.

She is tall but not as me, I can easily cover her up. She has long black silky hair, she has deep, intense yet warm brown eyes. She has soft and pouty full lips. She doesn't even have much make up on, yet she looks so beautiful. Fuck! She has the flawless body with a beautiful face. She is just so perfect, she can bring every man on his fucking knees.

If I could stare her the whole day, I would. I can see she is getting nervous and bites her bottom lip. Fuck........ But it suddenly hit me. What the fuck is wrong with me. I never take a good look at women and admire their beauty...... But why her?

"She is right, you need to calm down. Your brother needs you", my mother says from behind. Bringing me back to reality and the current situation. I wanted to say something, but I can't. What the hell. Unable to say something I just nod, without breaking the eye contact with her.

"Dr. White will show the way to the office, please follow her", the other doctor said. I see her name on her ID card of her coat. 'Dr. Kira White'.

She is the doctor..... Of course she is. My mother and grandfather accompany with me, I need to focus on my family right now, not on this woman.

She is walking in front of me I can't help but look at her ass.... Things I would to her pretty little ass. Fuck, Jason you need to focus on your brother right now.

"Please take your seats".

I can't help but I want to hear her sweet voice again. How am I so obsessed with her. So I question her.

"Will you just fucking tell us now", I shouted. Usually when I raise my voice, everyone gets scared to death. But she had a calm face that got me surprised. This is not what I used to get.

Generally people get scared and frightened by my vibe but it seems that she doesn't care about it. I dislike this feeling. I just met her about 15 minutes ago and what the hell is she doing to me.

Chapter - 5 Dinner?

K IRA

He is so rude. I mean I understand that he cares about his brother but still he can be a bit nice.

"With all due respect sir, your brother is out of danger and is totally fine. His skull was striked from front and back and his blood vessels were ruptured, by which it caused a severe brain injury. But we performed Craniontomy surgery and some fractured bones. Now he is in good condition", I explained them without looking him. Because if I did I won't be able to say anything. So I did my best to avoid his gaze.

"Will there be any complications futher", the old aged man said in a low voice.

"Hopefully no, but we need him to keep under observation for 2 weeks, so he doesn't have any further complications".

"When will he come around?", the lady asked.

"Maybe till tomorrow, he needs a lot of rest and make sure you don't stress him too much. Just try to keep him happy", I replied in a comforting tone by keeping my hand on hers.

"We will, you don't need to say that", the brute said. What's the problem with him, is he always like this?.

"Please just neglect him, he is just worried about his brother the woman said while giving me small smile.

"Please call me Julia, thank you for the cooperation. And sorry for everything that happened outside", she gave me a sad smile.

"You don't need to apologize Julia, It's a natural reaction."

Dr. Ron arrived to the office. He will futher discuss the details. My working hours has been completed and I should go home now. April , she must me waiting for me.

"I've got to get going, I look forward to our next meeting", I say and leave.

I'm really late today. I change my clothes and lock my locker. I hurry and got into the elevator. All I was thinking about was the gorgeous man. I would really like to see him again. Maybe I will ask him to hangout with m_____No. He is such an attractive man, he may already have a girlfriend or boyfriend......Who knows?

Why would he hangout with someone like me? Clearly he doesn't like me, the way he was speaking with me........ He is way out of my league.

I see annoyed April in front of me. I didn't realize, I was so caught up with my thoughts that I didn't know when I got out of the elevator.

"Did you plan having dinner with them", she was ready to attack me.

"I'm sorry they were just difficult to handle. Anyways, I want you to tell something", I was excited to tell her.

"Bitch, hope its worth it, now speak up".

You will not believe, I_______I was cut off by someone calling out my name.

****

Jason

I wanted her eyes in me, only at me. But she didn't even looked at me, like she completely ignored my presence. I kinda of hated this. Why isn't she looking at me? Why am I so desperate to have her eyes on me?

"We will, you don't need to say that", I say it just to grab her attention. I didn't realize, I was being so rude and mean to her. I wanted to test her limits. But she was so calm. How?

With all the interactions with her I can say that either she is controlling herself, or she is a strong woman. I started doubting myself for behaving bad with her. Never in my life I ever doubted myself but now.

Whatever she was doing to me, I don't want to stop it. Whether it was scaring me, but I don't want to stop it. I didn't realize when she left the room, it suddenly felt empty without her existence.

"You didn't have to be so rude to her. She saved Arlo, she was just trying to help us", my mother kept her hand on my shoulder comforting me and bringing me back to reality.

There is a sudden feeling in me to see her again, to have her presence around me. I want her all by myself. I get everything I want whether it is in business or a thing.What I want, I get. 'Kira White', You are mine and only mine.

"I know I shouldn't have mama, I will go and apologize to her", I kiss her forehead and leave to search her.

Where did she go, I searched her everywhere. I think she might be going home, so I rushed to the elevator. I pushed the ground floor switch. I hope she is still there. I'm really desperate to see her beautiful face again.

I reached the floor, my eyes were searching for her and there she was........talking with someone, her back was faced to me. She looked hot, even from back.

I called her name out loud. I could chant her name forever if I could.

****

KIRA

I think I know this voice. It is similar to________No, it can't be. I looked at April, her jaw is wide open and she has shocked look on her face. Does she knows him? No, it can't be. Then why is she so shocked?

I turn myself to face him. I think he just ran, because he was breathing continuously. Wait, what did I do? Did I do something wrong? Fuck........i think I did something wrong. I gather ny courage and spoke.

"Yes, Mr. Knight."

He stared me for couple of seconds and replied, "I'm sorry", in a low voice. I didn't expected that, I thought he was going to shout at me, remembering the past interactions.

"W-Why S-Sir?", I whispered. Shit, I'm stuttering and nervous.

"Call me Jason. I apologize because I shouldn't have behaved with you the way I did. You were nice and saved my brother in there. I'm really grateful for what you did", he said in a low calming voice.

"No, you don't need______", I was cut off by him again.

"I was certainly wrong. I want to invite you to have dinner with me tomorrow, in a way to apologize to you", he said with his gleaming eyes. Oh my god, did he just invite me to dinner.

"You don't need to, it's fine please______".

"She will come, I will make sure she does,", April interfere the conversation while giving me a side hug. What is she doing?

"April", I warn her. "I appreciate it, but I can't, I don't know you".

"You don't know me?", he questions me back.

"Yeah kind of", I replied.

"We will get to know each other than, if you agree for the dinner tomorrow", he said with hope in his eyes.

"Okay", I whisper.

"Good, I will pick you up after your work", he reached out his hand. I just nod and shake his hand. His hand is so warm. He is having huge hands compared to mine.

"But, she doesn't have your number", April again interfere our conversation. I just don't believe this woman. She is more eager than me.

"Ohhh I just forgot, thanks by the way". He gave me his phone, I reached out and type my number and gave it to him. He had a bright smile on his face.

"Well....... Good night then", he said.

"Good night Jason", I smile and leave.

My heart started doing a happy dance.Am I dreaming? If I am, i don't want to wake up. April was trying to say something, but I couldn't hear it clearly because of the crowd.

There were so many people gathered outside. It never happened before, and most of them were media.

"Why there is media all over here?". I question April.

"I knew you wouldn't know, Bitch did you know who is he?", April said in duhh tone.

"What he has to do with this?".

"Will you just let me complete. He is the one and only 'The CEO of Knight Enterprises, 'Jason Knight'. The Billionaire and the most eligible bachelor in the whole NYC. Thousands of women dream about him including me. Crazy woman, you don't know how how fortunate you are", she said it one breath.

OH MY GOD!!!!

Chapter - 6 - Dreams

JASON

I just fucking asked her out. I never hangout with any women in public. No, she is not just any women. She is special.

I remember the moment when I asked her out. The way she was calling me sir, I would so many things to her and her little ass.

She was nervous and she was stuttering. I like when people stutter when they are scared of me. But I don't want her to be sacred of me. When she was stuttering, I find it kinda cute.

And when she called out my name. Fuck, I just wanted to kiss her soft pouty lips so hard. Never my name sounded so sweet as she called me.

I thanked her friend. She should get a fucking reward, because of her I got her phone number. I can tell her friend was more excited than her.

The main important thing was she didn't know me. I mean, I'm kind of popular within the women and I always find women throwing themselves at me. She didn't knew me, this is new.

I didn't find her throwing herself at me. She was even ready to reject me, but I was saved from her friend. Yes, she definitely deserves a reward.

Why she didn't wanted to go out with me? Does she have any boyfriend? Even if she did, I would fucking kill him. The thought of her with any other man, makes my blood boil in anger. She is mine. I can't wait until tomorrow.

"Why are you so late, did you really apologize to her", my mother asked me.

"Yes mama, I did", I replied sitting next to her, outside the ICU.

"You should get some rest", grandpa said.

"You need to go for work tomorrow. We all are here just take the kids with you. You all need to rest. Please ", he said in low voice.

I've always listened to him no matter what. "Ok grandpa, call me if he wakes up or anything you need. Take Care. "

I drop them and reached home. I was relieved my brother is safe. All I could think was about Kira. I'm already imagining her on my bed naked and wet for me.

Shit, I see my dick is erect. I'm already hard. I'm gonna need some cold shower. I couldn't get her out of my head and even this erection.

The shower is on. My hand is on my dick moving up and down imagining her in the shower. I see, she is all naked in front of me. Water slips under her defined body.

She is on her knees, her hand is on my dick. Fuck, she looks so amazing in this position. She takes my dick in her mouth wide open all at once.

She sucks me hard and fast having her mouth wrapped around me. I don't think I would last anymore.

"Fuck baby, I'm so close", I moan and she picks up her pace going hard and fast and moaning my name.

I shoot my load of cum on the shower wall. "Fuck", I grunt. I'm already having wet dreams about her. I can't wait to make her mine.

____

I wake up again breathlessly in my bed. I cover my face with my hands. I take my time, and take deep breaths. 'No they can't hurt you anymore, I'm safe'. I have nightmares every night. I hug myself and sit on corner of my bed.

I get ready for work, early morning. I reached my building. My office is on 32th floor. My assistant gives me the details about today's schedule. She is an old women, her name is Marina. She is nice, does her job perfectly.

Before her, I had many other young women. They usually used to get naked in front of me, in my office. During my working hours, I only concentrate on my work. I preferred work more than women. So, I fired them all and decided to appoint her to avoid any distractions.

Lately, I'm thinking about her. How is it possible that I'm thinking about her 24/7? I'm imagining her on my desk bending all over down. Fucking hell, I need to control myself or I might fuck it all up before I'm able to start anything.

****

KIRA

I knew I saw him somewhere. I remembered now, I saw him on the magazine. He is the Billionaire Knight. I just made a fool out of myself. I couldn't believe he asked me out.

April was on top of the moon. She was just rambling non stop till we got home. I go to my room and fresh up. We were in the living room.

April opened her laptop and she searched him on google, I just don't believe her. I'm still trying to process everything.

"See, I told you he never dated anyone before. And now, he asked you out. I'm so happy for you. Wait, we need a fancy dress for you and my make up kit", she was jumping on the sofa continuously.

" April, he just invited me for dinner to apologize. If he has never dated any women, I think he's gay", I say it but I don't want it to be true.

"Don't jump conclusions Kira, ask him tomorrow and just spend your time with him. Finally, after so many years you are going on date", she keeps her hand on my thigh, trying to reassure me.

" But________

"No Kira. Just remember he is not like him. Give him a chance, maybe he is your end. "

"April, your thinking way to far", I let out a laugh.

"Bitch, just repeat after me. He is not like him", she holds my both hands in hers.

"He is not like him", I say in sad voice.

"Good, I'm so excited. My best friend is going out with the rich, hot billionaire 'Jason Knight ', she says and we both laugh out loud. I hope he is not like him.

____

I got up early in the morning. I'm all ready for my work. Maximus and Julius are staying with their dates , I might see them in the hospital.

I'm currently on my rounds for check ups on patients. My next round is with Arlo Knight. He was sober this morning. The media was still out there. I went to his ward with a nurse appointed with me.

I can see his whole family but not him. I was slightly dissapointed. I watch them, they were so happy for him. Just like a happy joint family.

"How are you catching up lately, do you have any pain", I check his pulse and other test reports.

"Wow, you are hot. Are you the one that saved my life babe? ", he smirks at me. I can tell he flirts with a lot of women.

"Well I'm one of them. You should really thank your family members, they all were here for you", I said with a laugh.

" Thank you everyone for being with me and saving me", he says it sarcastically and his one hand is in air. We all laugh at his actions. He is a joyful person to be and he remainded me of Maximus.

"You need a lot of rest and no movement. Their is a switch beside the bed, if you need anything just press the button".

"Yeah sure I will, if it means to see you again", he winks at me.

"Leave the poor girl alone Arlo, and just rest", his grandfather kinda saves me.

I don't know, when but it's already evening.April and I reached home and she started doing my make up and doll me up. I'm nervous. After few years, I'm going out with a man. Wait, is this even a date? I'm gonna go crazy.

He called me a few minutes ago, he is currently in hospital with his brother. He said he will pick me up. My hands are getting sweaty and my heart is beating fast.

Suddenly my doorbell ranged, April opened the door...............

Chapter - 7- First Kiss

K IRA

He is wearing a blue suit, he shaved his beard, and God his perfume smells so addicting. His mouth is wide open when he sees me and then shakes his head.

"Ahh-Um-I-You look stunning Kira, absolutely so beautiful", he blushed. He was stuttering. 'Cute'.

"Thank you, you are so hot, I-Um-I mean handsome. Shit, I'm sorry", I think I'm embarrassed of myself. He just smiles at me and thanks April. I don't know why?

"Shall we", he shows me the way.

" Y-Yeah", I take a last glance at April. She gives me a thumbs up. She even kept a condom in my purse. I mean..... What was she even thinking. I'm not planning to have sex with him.

We are outside of my apartment. He is having a black BMW car. Ofcourse he has, he is a billionaire stupid. He opens the door of the car. I get in. He sits beside me. We both don't say anything for minutes.

"Did you meet your brother?", I break the silence.

"Yes, he's doing great", he replied.

The car stops. We are front of fancy restaurant. He quickly gets out and opens the door for me. I slowly walk out of the car. He places one hand on my back, I flinch slightly and shows the way with his other hand.

We enter the restaurant, but the place is empty. A lady approaches us, "Sir, please this way", and leads the way. He takes out the chair for me.He is quite a gentleman.

"What do you want sir and ma'am?".

"My usual with red wine and", he looks at me. I'm already looking at the menu card. This is so costly restaurant, no wonder, no one is here.

"Roasted chicken please", I said to her. She nods and leaves us alone.

"You complained yesterday that we don't know each other. So let's start with introducing myself. My name is Jason Laszlo Knight. I'm CEO of Knight Enterprises and you are...? ", he says with a bright smile on his face.

"I think you took it more seriously ",I say it with a giggle.

"Ok......So my name is Kira Regina White. I'm a doctor and I work in CityMed Hospital as a surgeon, and thanks for inviting me", I smile.

"Hmm, are you from here?", he asked.

"No.....I came to NYC for job with my friend. It's been quite a few years now", I replied. I still had many questions in my mind, that I wanted to ask him. The dinner is served.

"It's strange, this place is not crowded with people", I eat my dinner.

"Actually, I booked the whole place for us. I'm not a social person. I usually don't go out", he just smiles at me. His smile is so beautiful.

"Ohh....Okay. Umm - do you have any girlfriend?", shit why did I asked that. He was taken back.

"I'm so__

"No, it's fine. I don't have any girlfriend. I never dated anyone yet", I drink the wine. I think that if he had never dated any women, then he must be a gay.

"No, I'm not a gay. I didn't found anyone who is worthy of my time", I almost choke my drink. How did he know what I was thinking? And he laughed. He just laughed. It was such a sweet laugh.

"Umm-Ah-so, am I w-worthy of your time? ", I was curious to know.

"You absolutely are", he answered and I blushed like a teenager.

We continued our conversation, we got to know about each other. I got to know what he likes and dislikes. I can say he was a little reserved and formal at first but later he just went with the flow.

I couldn't believe that he is 'Jason Knight', the billionaire. It was like I knew him before. I felt free around him. He.....He's.....I don't know but different, like a mystery. When I look in his beautiful blue eyes, they seem lost and I can sense pain.

No....Why would he be in pain. He is a billianore. I'm just overthinking.We finished our dinner with some desserts. We are on the way home. He is way more close than before, not that I'm complaining.

We reached my apartment. Before I can open the door, he quickly opens the door and stretch out his one hand. I accept it.

"Did you liked it? ", Jason asked.

"Yes, it was amazing. Thanks for the dinner".

"Pleasure is all mine. I still think you didn't accept my apology".

"No, I enjoyed your company and I have really accepted your apology".I hug him to reassure him. God he is so warm. I want to be in his embrace ...like forever. We break the hug, but we are still close to each other.

He was staring at me and he finally said, "Kira don't think I'm doing this for to just earn your apology, but I like to know more about you".

I just stared at him, I knotted my eyebrows in confusion. Did I heard correct? "W-What do you m- mean?", I was trying to take a step back but he was having different plans.

Without warning Jason grabs my wrist and tugs me into his chest. And then placing both hands on my waist tightly, he caged me, making sure I'm trapped within his arms.

He bends down and buries his face between the nape of my neck. His breath was teasing me and a shiver ran down my body. He started kissing my neck and I unintentionally tilted my head to give him more access. I lost my complete energy. My legs would have given out, if his arms weren't holding me tightly.

"Mhmm", I moan.I tired my best to stop it, but I can't. He was so addicting and I didn't want him to stop.

My chest was pressed against his. He sucked my skin. He started giving me open mouth kisses, and travelling his way up to my jaw. God, his lips are so addicting. I was craving for his lips.

He lifts his head and looked right in my eyes, "Can I kiss you Kira?", he asked in husky voice. We were so close, our lips were almost touching.

"Y-Yes", I replied. I just wanted his lips on mine. I can see the lust in his eyes. We both couldn't control ourselves anymore. He crashed his lips to mine ant I kissed him back. My hands were around his neck and his arms tightened more around my waist. I'm sure that's gonna leave a mark.

He is kissing me hard, we both fight for dominance but at last he wins. His tongue slid across my bottom lips. Giving him more access, I slightly open my mouth, he finds the opportunity and bites down my lip. A moan escaped from my lips. Whenever, our tongue collided with each other, a moan came out.

I grab his hair in my fistful hands. He just grunt out A voice. After few moments, he finally let go. We both were out of breath. I never knew kissing would be so intimate. We rest our foreheads.

It felt like a dream, heaven. I don't want him to let go, not after what happened. I open my eyes, he's already watching me with a bright smile on his face. Fuck, I kissed him.

"It was.....It was amazing", he said still keeping me caged amd my hands against his chest.

"Y-Yeah, I probably should go now", we finally are apart.

" Umm-when we can meet again?".

"Well, you have my number, right? ", I replied with a smirk and playful eyes.

"Good night Laszlo".

"W-What did you call me?", he was surprised.

"Laszlo, it's beautiful. I like it even more. If you don't w_____

"No, you can. Goodnight Kira", he said.

I'm so happy. After so many years I feel free.

Chapter- 8 Demons

J ason

I reached home. Today's day was so good. I recall everything that happen right from the hospital. After my work, I went to meet my brother.

Doctors told him to take complete bedrest. I enter the room, as always I see him flirting with the nurse. He flirts with everyone. He doesn't care about to the gender, whether male or female, he's always flirting. Yes, he's bisexual.

I clear my throat to grab his attention, "Oh there you are brother, I missed you so much", he fake crys. Drama queen. The nurse leaves.

"I'm glad you're okay. You got us all worried. I never thought I'd say it, but I missed you too", I sat on the chair beside him.

"You are in good mood. Wait.....You are not my brother. You never say that, especially to me. Oh my God, who's the girl? Tell me bastard!! ,he was shocked.

"OK-ok, she's.......she's one of the doctor's that saved your life", I said without looking at him.

"The hot one? Ahh......what was her name......Yeah,Kira White", he scratched his head.

"Yeah, how do k____anyways that's her", I never used to share anything with him but I did. Because I needed to share this with someone.

"I knew I liked her too. I mean who won't. Shit dude, she's so hot and that ass of h______

I cut him off, "Don't you dare complete the sentence or I won't be responsible for your other broken bones", I threatened him.

"Woah dude, I was just kidding. You like her, there's no chance I will come in between, unless you want me to...... ", he winks at me. I look at him in disgust. Yeah, he is completely fine. Later, I tell him everything about today's plan. He was completely surprised.

"Bitch, you are taking her on a date, within a day. Fuck man, I want to see this. My brother, who is always busy with work, is going out with a woman. She must be really special dude".

"My baby is really special".

"Fuck, you are whipped", he laughs at me. I punch his shoulder, he winced in pain, and we both laugh .

My file is ready and I don't have any meetings. There's still quite a lot of time, but I did not want my baby to wait, so I showed up early at her apartment. This is usually not my thing. I'm completely new at this, but Arlo gave me some tips. I hope it will help me.

————————————————

I rang her door bell. April opened the doors, behind her was my baby. Holy shit, what the fuck!! She was wearing an off shoulder red colour dress, upto her mid thigh. Showing her long and lean legs with a high pointed heels. Fuck me, her body was so perfectly defined in that dress.

And her ass,those sexy curves, and God her lips. I wanted to kiss her so badly,and throw her in the bed and rip her dress off her body. I wanted to hear her moans. I wanted to be buried inside her tight little pussy so deep and hallow, that she couldn't be able to walk for weeks.

I saw her she was staring at me, with her beautiful brown eyes. Her eyes trail down my whole body. Shit,I'm hard again. I don't want her to see that.

Please baby have some mercy on me.

Then we went to restaurant. I basically booked the whole restaurant fo us. I don't want anyone to disturb us. Whenever I go out, either there are media or the women flirting with me. I don't want anything to go wrong as this is my first date of my life.

She considered this as a date right? I need to tell her it is more than that. I have a file about her, but I want to hear it from her.

Soon, we finished our dinner and way back to home. I closed the distance between us. I was sitting close to her. I wanted her body to be pressed against mine.

When she was leaving, she just.......just hugged me. I personally don't allow anyone to touch me. It's true. I hate when someone touches me leaving my mama. I look down at kira........If it was not her, I don't know what would I have done. When she hugged me, I felt peace that I haven't known before.

I felt I don't need to hide myself anymore. I felt no more demons in me, and a sudden urge in me to hug her back. I did. I just dipped my head in her neck. Her smell was so fucking addicting. I couldn't stop myself anymore, I started giving her wet kisses on her neck and a sweet moan escaped from her lips. That only encouraged me more to suck her skin harder.

I asked her if I could kiss her. I pray she would say yes and she did. I just wanted her permission. I kissed her hard, and she kissed me back with same energy. I got full access of her mouth. I bite her lower lip, she moaned. My baby liked a bit painful.

I wanted to take further, my dick was throbbing in my pants. She tasted so sweet. She kissed my demons. But I know I should stop. I need to take it slow with her before I mess up everything.

We were finally apart from each other. I remember her calling my middle name 'Laszlo'. No one called me with my middle name, but coming out of her mouth sounded music to my ears.

———————————————

My heart is literally dancing. I'm feeling so good. I decided to message her.

Baby"Goodnight baby. Sweet dreams".

Baby"Baby, I don't regret kissing you".

I know she would be overthinking, so I messaged her.

I'm all alone in my house. I don't need any flings today and I don't think I will ever need them again. They were just meaningless, as I basically gave them pain and torture.

I sleep in my bed. My biggest fear is sleep. Because I always get nightmares everyday and I'm all alone to deal with it. Soon my sleep takes over.

WarningThe futher content consist of child abuse. Do not read if you're not comfortable with the description. You can read it when the content is over.

"You bastard, what did I told you? I don't want you to attend your rubbish school. How dare you didn't obey me".

"P-please.......I-I-I won't g-go anymore. Please, d-don't hit m-me again", I was on my knees begging for him.

"You need to be fucking punished brat", he grabs the steel rod from the room. He usually hits me with a wooden bat, but today he bought a steel rod. This is going to pain so much.

Tears were running down my cheeks. " Please, I will l-listen to you.....and o-obey your o-orders......don't hit me", I begged him continuously. A shiver ran down my spine.

He swinged the rod hard and fast on my shoulder causing me to fall on the ground. But he didn't stop. He was beating me continuously, mercilessly. I cried my lungs out, I cried for help but no one heard nor he stoped.

The content is over.

I woke up catching my breath again. I sat on the floor near the corner of my room. My hands covering up my ears and my head in my knees.

After some time, I decided to have shower. Why I'm not able to forget about him?

"He's gone. He won't hurt you again. You're fully grown up ass now", I say it to myself.

I came out of shower. I wrap the towel around my waist. I look at myself in the mirror.I see scars all over my body. Mostly on my chest, my torso. These are scars of wooden bat, steel rods, scars of knifes that were deeply cut within and even bite marks all over my body.

I'm so disgusted of my body. It's full of scars, that are awful. I started to cover my scars with make up. Yes, I do it everyday because I hate my scars. I don't want to even look at them.

Why would anyone want to be with me after watching my scars? Will Kira be with me, even after knowing my demons?

Chapter - 9 - Trust

****

Kira

"So... how did your date go", April didn't even allow me to enter home.

"It went good", I enter inside and sit on couch, trying not to blush and she takes a sit beside me.

I look at her. "W-We kissed".

"Oh my god, bitch you just hit the jackpot. I'm gonna tell this to everyone and the bitch Amy too!!!".

"No, you're not. April please don't do anything stupid. This will only cause problems".

"But______

"No April".

"Fineee. I'm happy for you. How was it though?".

"I'm not discussing this with you", I throw pillow at her.

I'm so happy. I'm just trying to think what happened. I fucking kissed him.

Thousands of questions arise. Are we going too fast? How can someone like him be with a ordinary girl like me. Is he just playing with me?Did he regret kissing me?".

God, I'm overthinking again. I should get some sleep. I got a message, it was from none other than the gorgeous man 'Laszlo'. I liked it even more than his first name. It's unique, so I saved his number as 'Laszlo'.

Laszlo"Goodnight baby. Sweet dreams".

Laszlo"Baby, I don't regret kissing you".

Fuck, does he have to be so sweet. He called me baby, it gave me butterflies in my stomach. I'm having a huge smile on my face. What are you doing to me Laszlo.

1 week later

I'm so tired right now. We just performed a surgery. I still have to go for my daily rounds.

Today Julius mood is not so great. Because he's boyfriend cheated on him. It's been few days, he's just reserved.

"Julius,why don't you accompany me for the rounds. You might feel better".

"Yeah.... Sure. I really need a distraction right now", he gets ready to accompany me.

We finally come to Arlo's ward. I gave Julius details about Arlo's condition.

"Ahh... There you are. You didn't come to visit me. I was waiting for you", he instantly sat straight from his sleeping position.

"Careful.... Well I was busy with the surgeries", I say and check his heartbeats.

"And.... who's this? My god aren't you a beautiful sight for my eyes", I look at him, but he was looking at Julius. I didn't knew he was interested in men as well.

I look up to Julius, he's already blushing. "I'm Julius.I-I'm here with Dr. Kira", he said in a low voice.

"Nice meeting you Julius. I'm Arlo. So Kira how was the date with my brother", he winked at me. Of course......he knew about the date.

"Dr.Julius, please check the futher reports, I will join later".

"Hey, you didn't answer my question ".

"Not now.Maybe some other time". I said and walked out.

I didn't meet Laszlo for days, because we both were so busy with our works. But we both chat and called each other everyday.

It's time for our lunch break. We always have lunch together in the canteen. "Guess what, Julius is having a new crush", I playfully look at Julius.

"What the fuck!! Who is the guy Julius?". Maximus was surprised.

"Arlo Knight", I wink at April and laugh.

"Wait, he's gay", Maximus questioned again.

"No, he's bisexual and he kinda.... liked Julius too", I replied.

"Wow!!! My best friend is dating Jason Knight and my other friend is having a crush on his brother. This day is getting better and better ", April laughed continuously.

We were chatting and a voice interrupted us. "Is this seat taken? ".I look up and see Lance standing with his food tray. "Sure Lance". I said. He took a seat beside me.

"So, what were you guys discussing? ", he asked while having his lunch.

"Nothing special, just sharing some gossips", Julius replied.

"Oh look, the bitch is on her way here with her two nincompoop friends", April said in a annoyed tone.

I don't even look back, because I know who she is. Amy Duncan, the one and only person in the world who hates me the most. I don't know the real reason, but I think it's because of Lance.

I explained her so many times that I don't have any interest in him, but still she doesn't believe me. I don't want to deal with this shit right now.

"Lance, sweetheart why are you not having lunch with us. Come with me", she took his hand practically dragging him with her.

"Amy you were busy, so I just_______

"I know it's because of her. When will you leave him alone", she points her finger to me. Fucking great. This woman blames everything on me. I don't understand how she got in medical field.

"She didn't do anything bitch. Talk to her like that again, I will kick your ass", April stood up to her level.

"Girls fight. I bet on April", Maximus laughed.

I don't want to deal with this right now. Suddenly my phone ring. I check my phone it's Laszlo. God, he is really my saviour.

"I need to take this call", I got up from my seat and walked out from the heated drama.

"Amy, she's already dating someone, just leave her alone", April said. "What!! Is she really dating someone?",Lance said. I heard them from behind but I just ignored them.

After going far at some distance I picked up his call. "Hey baby, are you free?Am I disturbing you?", why does he have to be so sweet.

"Quite opposite actually. So, what are you doing".Whenever I talk to him, I get butterflies in my stomach.

"I'm thinking about you. I have a meeting in few minutes. I thought it's best if I call you".

"Me too. I'm glad that you called me", I missed him too.

"I'm arriving hospital this evening, just wait for me okay".

"Y-Yeah, I will ", I said in a low voice.

"Great. Bye baby ", he ends the call.

Yes....I'm finally gonna meet him today. I forgot everything that happened a few moments ago, because he just changed my mood.

What is this feeling? Is it lust or am I just attracted to him? After my last relationship, I didn't trust anyone. It was difficult. My ex boyfriend stalked me for years. Those days with him were painful. I trusted him, but he just.........

"Ok Kira just stop thinking and now focus on your work ", I say it to myself.

I hope I'm doing right this time by trusting Jason.

Chapter - 10 - Patience

Jason

I'm currently working on the files, in my office. I'm working continuously for days. I didn't even met my baby after that night. We both were busy.

I have another fucking meeting in few minutes. I'm working continuously for days because I'm going to take some days off. I don't want to meet her only for few hours. I want to spend my whole day with her.

I never took any day off, but only for her. Only for my baby. I still have some time. I decided to call her. I hope she's not busy.

"Hey baby, are you free? Am I disturbing you?", I ask her.

"Quite opposite actually. So what are you doing?", I could hear her voice whole day.

"I'm just here thinking about you. I have a meeting in few minutes. I thought it's best if I call you".

"Me too. I'm glad that you called me", it was relief to know that she missed me too.

"I'm arriving hospital this evening, just wait for me okay", I really want to see her.

"Y-Yeah I will", she said.

"Great, bye baby ", I say and end the call. Okay, I will finish the meeting as soon as possible.

———————————

It's been three fucking hours now. Still the meeting is going on. Enough, I can't do this anymore. So I cancelled the meeting. They were wasting my time and energy.

I arrived hospital late. I met my brother. He's really a pain in my ass. He just couldn't leave me alone, but I some how managed and escaped from him.

I called Kira, she said she is near the reseptonisit. I wait there. I managed themedia out there and made sure they didn't know about my arrivals.

Everyone down here is looking at me. Especially women are eye fucking me. I have my bodyguards with me for 24/7 but not for my first date with Kira. I didn't wanted her to be uncomfortable.

Someone tap my shoulder from behind. I turn around and see her. There she is, my baby, with a cute smile on her face. She was going to hug me, but someone called out my name.

"Mr.Knight, it's a pleasure seeing you here", this fucker again. He just interrupted my precious moment with Kira.

"Ahh, I see Dr. White is also here, didn't your working hours got complete? You should go home now rather than flirting with Mr. Knight. I will speak with you tomorrow", he said in a angry tone.

I will kill this fucker right now. How dare he speak with my baby like that? He needs to be teached a fucking lesson and I will make sure he does.

"Kira wait outside, I want to have a word with Dr.Ron", I whisper to her.

She nods and walk out. I turn to him. "Shall we talk somewhere private", I try to control my anger. "Yeah sure. This way Mr. Knight".

We are in a private ward. I inform my bodyguards to stay outside, and don't allow anyone to enter the room. We sit down opposite to each other and he removes a bottle of cheap alcohol.

I don't say anything."Sorry for what happened outside. You already know that these worthless bitches doesn't know their limit. They see a rich man and are ready to become a fucking whore", he said with a disgusting laugh.

That's it. I got up from my seat, grab a ink pen from the holder and prick the pen in his knees. He cries out in pain. His cries bring me relief to my nerves.

"If you say anything about Kira with that disgusting mouth of yours, I swear this pen would be in your fucking throat", I raised my voice. Pool of blood was coming out from his knee.

"Never speak to her like that again. Remember always treat her nice", I dig the pen deeper and deeper in his flesh.

"P-Please...... I-I-I'm sorry...... I won't do it ever a-again".

"Good, and yeah she won't be attending the hospital for some days. You won't say anything to her. Do you understand?".

"Do you understand", I shout.

"Y-Yes, u-understood ", I leave the pen in his flesh. My hand is covered with his blood, I wash it out. I was ready to leave, before leaving I turn to him,

"No one should know what happened here. If it gets out, it will be your last fucking day on this earth", I give him a warning and he looks scared as shit.

I walk ot of hospital in hurry. I wasted a lot of time. Kira would be waiting for me. I look out for her, she was sitting on bench which is quite near from Hospital.

She is sitting alone on bench at night waiting for me. I tell my bodyguards to go and bring my car.

"Is this seat taken", she looks at me, and gives me a smirk.

"No, it's only reserved for you". I sit close bedside her. I hold her left hand and kiss her knuckles.

"What did you two talk?".

"You don't need to worry about him. He won't say a word to you", she smiles at me.

"You shouldn't have______

"Shhh.....", I put my finger on her lips.

"You look tired. Do you need something?".

"Yeah, I had too much work today".

I scan her face she looks tired, but she didn't wanted to show me, and I made her wait for me this late. I'm so stupid.

"Let's get you home then".

We reached her apartment. I opened the car door for her. I like to do things for her. Only for her. I want to spend more time with her. She looks up at me.

"Do you wanna come inside? April and my other friends went to the club. They will be late tonight. So.....? ". It's like she read my mind. Yes.

"I thought you will never ask",I follow her behind.

We enter her apartment and she closes the door. "I'm sorry, it's messy here. It's not as great as compared to yours, but this is only I could afford", she gives me a sad smile.

"Don't be. I don't care about anything, as long as I'm with you", she blushes.

"Will you stop being so sweet now", she giggles and I laugh.

She takes my hand and leads the way to the couch. I sit down and she lays her head on my chest. I hold her and tucked a strands of hair behind her ear.

"Why didn't you go out with your friends?", I asked her.

"Spending time with you, has become my new hobby", I have a wide smile on my face.

"Are you hungry?".

"Yes, are you going to cook something for me?".

"Of course Laszlo, you get some rest while I prepare something for you", she gets up.

"I'll help you, come on", I go after her.

"Wait, you can cook? ", she had a surprised face.

"I know how to cook, but I don't usually do it. But I'm willing to do it for you", I remove my jacket and roll up shirt sleeves, and tie the apron around.

"Wow, the great businessman, 'Jason Knight', is cooking in my kitchen. What a beautiful sight for my eyes", she winks at me.

"You're lucky because I'm cooking or I would've kissed the living daylights out of you".

"What if I want that", she gets on the kitchen counter.

Baby, why are you testing my fucking patience.

Chapter - 11 - Trip?

KIRA

"What if I want too", I sit on the kitchen counter. I wanted to push him futher.

I don't know how we ended up in this position. He was between my legs standing and kissing me. My arms were around his neck. There was no air to pass between us.

He started kissing my jaw slowly and then trailing way down to my neck, I wrapped my legs around his waist. He started giving me open mouth kisses and suck my skin hard. He was doing it all over my neck, I realized he was marking me.

"Mhmm.....Laszlo", I moan his name and he started to suck harder.

My hands automatically travelled down to his shirt. I opened few buttons, but he stopped my hand and kept my hand around his neck again. He finally leaves my neck and looks up to me.

"I would love to continue this, but I have to feed you first", he winks at me and starts cooking again. How can he leave this in middle? I wanted his lips on mine.

"It smells so good", I said.

"You gonna like it even more when you taste it", he said while serving me some pasta.

"Mhmmm... ", I moan when I take a bite.

"Baby..... Don't do that", I chuckle and ate the food. It's really so good.

"We get it, you are really a good cook".

We finished dinner. "I want to talk something serious now", I look at him and gave my full attention.

"I-I.... I planned a t-trip for us in Maldives", he doesn't look at me. He keeps looking down. Did he said trip?

"Jason.... You want to go on a trip with me?", I used his first name to grab his attention. He stares at me and slowly nod.

"But I don't_______", I was cut off

"I know, I'm sorry I didn't asked you first. But I wanted to surprise you and spend some time with you. I don't want to spend half evenings, I want to spend my whole day with you", he gives me a sad smile.

My whole heart melts. He planned this for me, for us.

"I don't k-know what t-to say. It's really nice of you, but I don't think I would get two weeks off from Hospital". It's true, they barely give us some holidays.

"I've managed everything. You don't need to worry about your work, I discussed it with Dr. Ron. He said he doesn't have any problem. I won't take no as your answer ", he holds my hand.

"Did he really said that? ", I couldn't believe because Dr. Ron is very strict and doesn't allow anyone to take a day off without genuine reasons.

"Yes, now please say something because I'm dying here woman!!!", I giggle and kiss his hand and my thumb rubs back and forth on his hand.

"I would love to spend time with you Laszlo, but don't you think it's too many days. I mean I can't afford that_______".He doesn't allow me to complete and kisses me.

"As I said it before I've managed everything baby, you just need to say yes", he peck my lips again.

"So when are we leaving? He looks surprised and then lifts me up, I wrap my legs around him and throw my head back in laughter.

"I promise you won't regret it. We will leave tomorrow evening ok. You can pack your bags until tomorrow", he still holds me up.

"It's late, you should stay", I play with his hair, I really don't want him to leave. I like the way our bodies are pressed against each other.

"You don't need to tell me twice. Where's your room?", I show him the way while I'm still in his arms. We enter my room and sits on the bed.

"Wait here, I'll bring some comfortable clothes for you", I go to Julius room, because recently he bought some clothes in sale which were too loose for him. I bet it will fit Jason perfectly.

I went back to him. He was still seated in the same place like a good boy. I give a T-shirt and sweat pants.

"Where did to you get this clothes from?", he asked while removing his shirt. It was sexy, the way he slowly unbuttoned his shirt and finally the shirt was off his body.

Fuck me!! He was indeed a gorgeous man I've ever seen. He is having eight packs and his muscles are defined so perfect which made him even more sexier. Who can guess he's having such a hot body underneath those business suit.

"You didn't answer my question baby? Are you done checking me out", I shake my head, control Kira.

"Umm... It's my friend's clothes.Actually he and his brother kinda live here with us. They are twins", I said not looking at the half naked man in front of me.

He comes closer to me. He takes my chin and forced me to look up at him. "You live with two men. That's not good baby. I don't like sharing what's mine", he was damn serious. He said mine.

"You got it all wrong", I laugh at his possessiveness.

"Baby I'm serious and you're laughing!!", he said cupping my cheeks on his both hands. I keep my hands on his chest, he suddenly flinched. Why? I take my hands down, but he brought them back on his chest again.

"Julius is a gay and Maximus doesn't even stay here that much".

I slowly take my hand to his cheek and rub it slightly. "You don't need to be worried about them. They're just my friends Laszlo and I think you should dress now. I will change in bathroom", I said.

"They better be. Now go before I throw you over my shoulder", I can hear him laughing at me.

I changed my clothes and came out. He's already sleeping in bed and was waiting for me. Even in casual clothes he is looking so handsome.

I climbed the bed and lay down beside him. He reached out his arm and wrapped me around him. I started kissing his neck slowly.

"Not now baby", he kisses my nose. I pout my lips in disappointment.

"I know. I'm controlling myself too. But I want you to enjoy this trip with me. But I promise you these two weeks I'm gonna pleasure you and your body and when I'm done with you, you won't be able to walk for weeks ", he promised me weeks filled with pleasure.

I can't wait to go on this trip. My head is on his chest and he kisses my forehead. I draw small patterns on his chest with my fingers. I look up to him, his already asleep.

I know he works hard and also his work is full of stress but still he manages to take out some time for me. I appreciate it. He looked so peaceful while sleeping. I press a kiss on his forehead, in response he holds me more tightly. I rest my head again. He lives in a huge bunglow and fancy hotels but still he is here with me.

———————————

There is a huge bang on the door, waking me up. "Get up Kira, we are gonna be late", there she is. Everything was going so perfect but not anymore.

"Yeah, I heard you", I said. I still didn't tell her anything. I didn't even know when did they came. I look at LaszloHe's still sleeping. I lean down and kiss his nose, "Wake up sleepyhead", I started kissing his jaw.

He opens his eyes and gives me his bright smile. "Good morning Baby", he kissed me. He nuzzles his face in my neck". April and my friends are outside, waiting for me. I need to tell them about our trip". I said. He just hums and nod his head.

I had spare toothbrush, we freshen up. He wore his suit that he was wearing yesterday. He didn't shower because we were already late, but I convinced him to stay up for breakfast.

I take his hand in mine and open the door, "At last you showed________", April was ready to shout at me, but when she saw Jason she stops. Maximus and Julius are shocked too.

"Holy Jesus, Jason Knight walked from my front door ", Maximus said.

"Umm... Hii guys can I join you all for breakfast?",Jason broke the silence.

"Of course sir, It will be our pleasure ", Julius said taking out a chair for him. April was looking at me as she was ready to kill me. I go closer to her, "You better explain me later, when he's gone", she gives me a death glare and serves a plate for Jason.

"I can't believe we are having breakfast with you sir", April said.

"Please call me Jason", he smiles. I take a sit beside him. We have our breakfast. Everyone was so keen to speak with Jason. He gets a phone call. I think it's about his business , he ends the call and looks at me.

"I have one urgent meeting in some hours. When it ends I will call you, till then pack your bags. I will pick you up by evening okay. Bye baby", he kissed me.

"Thank you for having me here ", he says and everyone thanks him too.

I close the door. I turn and find all three are standing, folding their arms, ready to kill him. 'Please God help me'.

"Did you both had sex last night?"."Why did he said to pack your bags?"."Are you both serious about this relationship?".First April, Julius and then Maximus. I told them everything, they were shocked.

"Wow, you are going to Maldives. I'm so jealous right now", Maximus said.

"I guess happy journey. I'm gonna miss you so much Kira", Julius gives me a hug.

"Bitch, we need to go shopping right now", April dragged me out. I laugh at her actions.

I can't wait for this trip.

Chapter - 12 - Sweet Taste

JASON

I finally asked her and she said yes. I'm so happy right now. Last night was so different than the other nights. Shit, last night I wanted her so badly, but I controlled myself for her.

Because I'm gonna show her how perfect she is. I will make sure this two weeks will be perfect for us. Last night was a proof that she is different. I've never slept so peacefully before, hell I was also not used to cuddling.

We fit so perfectly together, her warm body against mine. I didn't had a nightmare last night. How? I always had nightmares at night.

The pain that I had was gone last night. She is special to me and I will never let her go. I have meeting right now, they are lucky because I am in a good mood.

I have a smile on my face, that's not going off. My driver was shocked when he opened the door for me. I walk to my building, everyone is glaring at me but my smile is still there. They are not used to see a smile on my face, because I always have a serious look on my face.

I'm currently in the meeting. I can't concentrate on the meeting, all I think about is Kira. Will she be able to take my pain away completely? Or will I cause her more pain?Once she knows the truth about me, would she leave me? I don't want her to. It's not the right time, I don't want to mess up anything. God, when did I started being this cheesy.

After the meeting I went home, my bags were already packed. I had this planned for so many days now. I called Kira and told her to get ready. I inform my family that I'm out for two weeks alone. I don't want to tell them now.

I'm currently waiting for her near her apartment. She comes down with her bags. "I'm sorry I'm late, I went for shopping", she said. "You could've told me, we would have gone for shopping", I kiss her forehead and hold her close to me.

We go to the airport. I managed all the media, so they didn't get any news. "We didn't book flight tickets. What are we gonna do?", I laugh at her.

"Baby we are going in my private plane", I take her hand in mine and kiss her knuckles. We enter the private plane.

"Oh my god, it's so beautiful"."It also has rooms, if you are tired", I said.

"No, I want to be with you", she holds my hand. "Baby, it's 17 hour long flight. Come on baby, I will take you after our dinner", I'm so excited for this trip. She's gonna love it.

She was tired and she is now sleeping peacefully on my chest. She is so precious for me. How did she become so important for me in matter of few days? I never spend holidays with my own family.

I give her fishy kisses all over her face."Wake up, we are going to land in 15 minutes", she yawns and gives me her morning smile. She squeals and move out of bed. I chuckle, "Baby slow down", I go behind.

She looks out of window. The view was so breathtaking. "Come on now, sit down we still have 15 minutes", she was going to sit beside me but I pulled her on my lap.

She was comfortable, in this position my dick grew more harder. She felt it too, she looks at me and I smirk. We made safe landing on the airport and I kept her close to me.

I booked hotel to stay in, of course only one master bedroom. She was surprised to see the room. I would do anything to have the smile on her face. The room also had a beautiful view.

We got ready for beach. I wore shorts and a loose T-shirt. I don't want to go in the water, because the make up will go off my body. So, I will try not to go in.Kira loves beaches, so I planned this.

She was wearing shorts, god those sexy legs are gonna kill me one day. It is bright sunny day. She removed her clothes, she was teasing me. She wore a red bikini. God, this woman is seriously trying to kill me.

I sat down looking at her, she is so beautiful. She came back running to me. "Come on, you should enjoy this", I kiss her passionately, "I don't like beaches", I replied and she had a frown on her face and I laugh.

I showed her the island, we had amazing seafood breakfast. Time went so fast, it was already evening, she was tired on the first day itself. I didn't want anyone to disturb us so I ignored my business calls.

She was reading a book for me in bed. She loves to read and I like to listen her voice. I grab the book from her hands, "Hey, give it back", she giggles.

Warning Mature content ahead

"I need some attention too baby", I started kissing her jaw but not kissing her lips, I like to tease her.

"Jason please", she moans grabbing my hair."Patience baby do you know what I'm gonna do with you?". I keep assaulting her neck. I bite and suck down on her soft skin. In response she just tilt her neck giving me more access.

"You make me so hard when you moan", I started undressing her. "I'm gonna eat your your pussy and when I'm done you would be cumming so hard only with my mouth and myfingers ".

I rip of her shirt and then bra, revealing her breasts. They stand aching for my attention. I grip one of them, I suck her nipple hard and give same attention to the other one.

I take off her jeans and throw them on the floor. I rip her lacey underwear too. So beautiful. I stroke her sensitive pussy with my fingers.

"Jason please", she moans loudly. "No baby, I want something more", I tease her clit, stroking it more and more and bringing her to the edge and then stop.

I do it again and again torturing her and not giving her a chance to release. "Laszlo p-please", she moans out loud. This is what I needed to hear from her.

"I can't believe these pretty moans are for me and this pretty little pussy of yours too, tell me what you want baby".

I kiss the way down without breaking the eye contact. I kissed her inner thighs and move my face closer to her vagina.

"So beautiful, smell so nice", I used my fingers to rub the clitoris and then stuff my face between her thighs.

I started to lick her clitoris. "D-Don't stop", she moans harder.

We are just getting started baby.

Chapter - 13 - Complete pleasure

Warning The futher scene contains mature content you can read it after the content is over.

KIRA

Oh my god!!! It's really happening. Jason is between my thighs, eating me out. He started licking all around my clitoris. He teased them enough and the pressure of his tongue on my clitoris is really hard and fast.

He increases the speed and pressure, and my body responses to it. "Fuck... Keep doing that", I grab his hair tight in my hands, guiding him way more inside.

"You taste so sweet, I can't get enough of you", he grunts but doesn't stop. "You are so sweet baby, don't you dare cum without my permission. I'm still not finished with you", he started stroking again with his fingers and sucking my pussy at same time.

"Deeper", I grab him by my legs. I never felt this feeling. It's complete bliss. He adds a finger inside my vagina and moves it slowly in and out.

"Ahh... Mhmm...", I strech my head backwards. Fuck, he is really expert at this. He knows how to pleasure a woman perfectly, just with his mouth and fingers.

Soon, he adds a second finger inside me, while circling my clitoris with his thumb. Oh god, I don't think I can last anymore. "Do you like it baby? You like it when I suck and finger you at the same time?".

I'm loving it. I like it even more, when he's talking dirty. "Tell me, or I will stop it right now". No, he wouldn't do that.

"Y-Yes.... I love it",I said. He fasten his speed. With other hand he grabs my nipple and plays with it. He started curling his fingers, when he found my G-spot.

"L-Laszlo please, I c-can't ", I was in complete pleasure. I couldn't even complete the sentence. "Cum baby, cum for me", he says as he bites my clit.

"Ahh.... Laszlo", I hold him as tight as possible. I didn't even thought I would cum so hard with just his fingers. He sucks every drop of cum and cleans me out. He is having a huge grin on his face.

He travelled his way up to me. I was so embarrassed, realising what just happened. I was not able to look at him, I looked the other way.

He grabbed my chin with his fingers and made me look up to him. He kissed me hard. I tasted myself on him. "Stop overthinking baby, I loved every moment of it. You don't need to be embarrassed", he said and kissed my forehead.

I don't know how, but within few days this man changed everything. He made me feel safe around him. He cares about me. I trust him so much, that I'm willing to try this with him.

I started removing his pants but he stops. "No baby, you are tired. We don't have to do it. It's okay", this is it. This made me want him even more.

"I trust you. I want to this", I started kissing his neck. I switched positions, as I was on top of him. I take off he's shirt, my hands roamed around his beautiful body. I look at him. We both stare at each other, "I want you Laszlo", I whisper in his ear and bite his earlobe.

"Are you sure, I don't want to hurt you", he said in a low voice.

"I'm sure", I kissed his nose. I removed his pants. He turns me over,"Remember baby, I'm the one in charge ", he smirks at me. He kissed me all over my face which made me laugh.

He removed his underwear, his dick was already hard. Oh my god!!! Never in my life I saw a penis this long. Not only long but also thick. I'm scared after seeing his dick. I look at him, "You are too big, I don't think it will fit", I said.

He cupped my cheek, "Don't worry about it, just look at me", he said while kissing my forehead. "Condom.... I don't have a condom", he sighed resting his forehead on mine.

"I have one in my purse", I whisper. I have it because of April. She always keeps it in my purse.

He gets it from my bag and tore the packet with his mouth. It was sexy to watch. Luckily it was his size. He's on top of me again. He kisses me passionately.

"Baby, just look at me, it might hurt a little but it will feel good baby I promise".

I was not a virgin, but I was feeling like one. I looked at him, but I felt his tip entering inside me. My mouth opens, and I moan out loudly. He holds me as tight as possible and continues to thrust inside me.

Tears were streaming down my eyes. He was really really big. He kissed my tears and swallowed my moans by kissing me deeply. He thrust me in and out slowly, but he's not fully inside me. Why?

I grab him by my legs, to be completely inside me. "Please Laszlo, I want you. Be yourself with me", I started moving with him. He's completely inside me and allows me to adjust his size. I moan his name out loudly.

He thrust now become more hard and fast. The room is filled with my moans and his grints. "Fuck..... Baby you feel so good", he grunts. "J-Jason I think I'm....".

"I know", he said and rides me faster. "Cum with me baby", he moans. I released my cum. Our breathing is the only voice we could hear.

"Baby on your fours now ". Does he not get tired? I follow his instructions. He fucks me from behind.

I think it's over one hour. I've cum for four to five times. He cums with me. I'm really fucking tired. He lays down beside me, holding me tightly.

Our bodies is covered with sweat and our heavy breaths. Fuck... I just had sex with him, and I fucking loved it. "That was amazing", he said and kissed my forehead. I really love his forehead kisses.

I look up to him,"I really like you Laszlo", I look deeply in his eyes. He cupped my face and kissed my nose. "I like you too baby. You have become really important person in my life". I'm really tired so I just nod. My eyes close automatically and I sleep on his chest.

The mature content is over

Next few days were perfect. We both are enjoying it so much. He holds me like I'm really precious to him. We enjoyed sightseeing and we are now having late night camping near the beach. I sit in front of him and he holds me. I rest my head back on his chest and he kissed my shoulder blade.

"Baby, I want to know more about you", he said while I was playing with his hands. "What do you want to know about me?", I laughed at him.

"Anything. Did you had a boyfriend? ", I straightened my back after hearing his question.

"There is nothing to know about it", I said. He kissed my shoulder blade again. "Baby, you can share it with me", he reassures me.

Do I want it to share it with him? Yes. I don't want to hide anything from him. Even if it means to share my past with him.

Here goes nothing. "I was in medical college, when I met him..... ".

Chapter -14 - Her past

J ASON

This few days with her had been my best days of my life. I don't want this trip to end. I want her in my life forever. She adds a meaning to my life. She is my peace.

We are currently camping late night at beach. Her back is faced to me and I'm holding her in my arms. J want to know everything about her. I wanted to know if she had a ex boyfriend.

When I asked her, she was not comfortable. There was a sudden change in her mood. Why? I reassured her. I kept on kissing her shoulder.

She is now calm. She starts speaking, "I was in medical college, when I met him..... He's name is Charles Williams. We met in a club a few years ago. At start, he was really sweet. We used to go on dates. I thought I would be happy with him, as he was the definition of perfect", she said.

I was really jealous. I didn't like how she talked about the guy. I was getting tensed. She senses my uncomfortness and holds my hand and kissed it.

"He was good at first. But later, he slowly started changing. He started shouting at me. He used to be angry at me without any reason.... And one day he slapped me", she stopped. She hold my hand tightly. I was angry at him.

"I was shocked. I didn't knew what happened. I decided that I can't live with someone who raises his hands on me. I should've left him before but I thought that I love him. I was so stupid right?", she said and laughed slightly.

"You left him?", I asked her. "I tired to leave but he blackmailed me. He fixed a camera inside my room, I didn't knew about the camera. He was having my nude photos and recordings. He said if I do something that would upset him, he would leak the videos and the photos".

"It started getting more worse day by day. He used to hit me unnecessarily. It was really painful", she buried her face in my chest.

I can't believe the nerve of that guy. My blood was boiling in anger. How dare he hurt my baby. He is gonna pay for what he did and I will make sure he does. I can feel her tears on my chest. He somewhat remainded me of a person I hated the most.

She looks at me, I wipe away her tears with my thumb and kiss her forehead. "I wish we would have met first", I said and I really mean it.

"How do you escaped from him? ", she has already suffered so much.

"I escaped when he was drunk.He used to punch me, bang me on the walls. It was really painful Jason.I asked April for help. I couldn't handled it anymore".I rub her back continuously and kept kissing her cheek.

"She saw my scars and helped me out. Her uncle is a cop. With his help, Charles got arrested and destroyed all the videos. I thought it was all finished but only after few months, he kept on stalking me. I travelled from place to place. But he always used to get my information. So, I decided to move to another country. I came to NYC with April".

I'm going to kill this fucker. Wherever he is, I would find him and make him pay for his mistakes. He really committed a big mistake in his life.

"You still have scars?"."No, they faded away with time", she showed me her arm, it was fade scar, it couldn't be noticeable.

"What about your parents?", I asked. "It's a story for another day", her answer was short so I didn't pushed her more.

"It's okay. I'm with you now. Nobody's gonna hurt you, you're safe with me baby". We rest our forehead against each other. I will not let anyone hurt her anymore.

"I always had the fear that one day he will find me again and cause me a lot of painI felt trapped. But, when I met you, I finally feel free", I open my eyes, her eyes are still closed. She kissed my cheek.

"Laszlo, can I ask you something?", she said. I just nod at her question.

"Do you have nightmares everyday?", I was taken back when she asked this question. I was not expecting this. How did she know?

"How do you know?", I questioned her back. She cupped my cheeks in her both hands. I rest my face in her hands and close my eyes.

"Last three-four nights you sleep talk, you were shivering, scared and your body was covered with sweat", my eyes are still closed. I don't want to look at her. Did she heard everything? Will she leave me now? Did she saw my scars? No I covered it up, and it is waterproof.

She kissed my closed eyes, "You were crying baby, you were shaking with fear", I open my eyes. She called me baby.

"Why didn't you told me before? I'm sorry I disturbed you", I look down. She makes me look up to her, "I thought you had a bad dream. You didn't disturbed me, I held you every night, then you used to calm down", she said.

She didn't saw my scars, but she helped me every night. This is the reason, why I don't remember anything, because she helped me.

"I...I....", I can't do this. She will leave me. I can't risk that. I don't know what I'll do without her. No no no..... I can't do this.

"K-kira.... Actually..I-I"."Hey it's okay. I know you're not ready. I don't want to force you. But just remember whenever you're ready I will be there with you", she rubs her thumb slowly on my cheek.

"Thank you baby", I kissed her knuckles and I kiss her. I try to change the topic. "I have an idea, do you want to hear it out", I said.

"Tell me Mr. Knight. What idea do you have? ", she giggles.

"Ok.... I think we should have sex on beach, here right now", I smirked at her. "No, I don't think that's a good idea"."Why?I want you right now", I pout my lips at her.

"We are having sex non-stop. We did it a few hours ago", it was true. When I had a taste of her, I couldn't stop myself. We both couldn't control ourselves anymore.

My hand travelled down, inside her panties. "Liar, you are so wet baby. Always fucking ready for me", she moan clenching my shirt.

She pushed me down on beach. She sat on me and removed my shirt. "You turn me on baby, I don't think anyone has ever gotten me this horny without actually touching me before", she removes her top.

Fuck, I like this playful side of hers. " I want to feel how wet you are", we had sex on beach. I love to have her body against mine.

I want her in my life forever beside me. She tries to bring a different person out of me and I like that.

It's been two weeks, and we both are really happy. It felt like heaven. Her smile lightens my day. I want it to make official. I want everyone to know that she's mine and I'm hers.

But I want to handle her ex boyfriend Williams or Charles, whatever his name is. I want to find this motherfucker before I make it official with her or he would cause more problems.

We are currently in my private plane flying back. She sat beside me and plays with my hands.

"Baby, will you be my girlfriend? ".

Chapter - 15 - I need you

K ira

"Baby, will you be my girlfriend? ", I'm surprised. He really wants me to be his girlfriend.

"Are you sure about it. I don't have any problem if you______".

"I want you and only you. I'm hundred percent sure about it", he looks at me. "I would love to be your girlfriend but I have one condition".

"Really!!!Thank you baby", he kissed all over my face and I giggle.

"Hey, will you listen to me now", I stopped him and he laughs at me. "I don't want media to know about us", I don't want Charles to know about me. I don't want him to destroy my happiness. I hope he says yes. I need time.

"I have no problem baby", he kissed me non stop and I giggle at his actions.

We landed on the airport and then we are currently in his car. But it's not the way to my home. "Laszlo, we going in the wrong direction, my apartment is on the other way", I look out of window.

"I know, we are going to my home baby", he shrugs. "Why? You don't________

"For once in your life, will you stop questioning me woman. Let me complete", he holds my hand.

"We are going to my home because you are gonna stay tonight with me, and I won't take 'no' as a answer. Tomorrow I will drop you at work in morning. So.... I answered all your questions baby ", he said and kissed my forehead.

I get out of the car, oh my god!! Fuck, his house is huge, definitely a big mansion. I can see numerous vehicles parked around. He holds my waist tightly and shows me the way. His living room is so big, more than the size of my entire apartment.

He has many maids in his big mansion. A lady came and greet us. "You are home Jason, I'm really happy to see you", she gives her joyful smile and she sees me.

"Oh my god, you brought a young lady with you. She's so beautiful", she hugs me and I hug her back. "Kira, she's Eden , she takes care of everything in the house. Eden she's Kira my....my girlfriend", he blushed.

"Jesus finally, I was tired of you and your brother bringing your flings____ _"."Eden, Kira is tired I would like her to take to my room", he said in stern voice.

Flings? Does he always do that? Am I just a temporary thing to him? Does he takes every women for vacations? Am I just a plaything to him?

I was thinking hundreds of questions in my mind . I didn't realize we were in his room. His room is really beautiful, fancy but it's not the answer to my questions.

"Baby don't. Look at me", he cupped my cheeks. "I know you are over-thinking. Do you trust me?", he asked. Do I trust him? Yes, I do. I just nod at him.

"It was before when I met you. It never meant anything", he looks down. "What I mean to you?", I really wanted to ask him, I don't want to be broken again.

"Am I just a play______".

"Don't you dare complete the sentence. Just don't. Have I not done enough to prove you that you are important to me. I'm never been like this with anyone but you. You make me feel things I never felt. Hell, I never allow any women to touch me leaving my mother. You are first woman who has touched me and you will be my last", I look in his eyes he's telling the truth.

Because spending last few days with him. I can say he is very distant person. Everyone is scared of him. He is still cupping my cheeks. "Why me Laszlo?". I want to know what he sees in me.

"You bring the best out of me. Nobody makes me feel the way you make me feel. It is you. It is fucking you. I cannot describe it anymore. You are the only one that I'll ever want. I belong to you. You are the only thing that matters. You are my good", he closed his eyes.

"If I could give you one thing in life, I would give you the ability to see yourself through my eyes, only then you would realize how special you are to me", I can feel tears on my cheek and I realize I'm crying. No one has ever said me that.

He wipes my tears with his thumb. I can see he is panicked. "Baby, please don't cry, I'm sorry", I kissed him, he lifts me up and I wrapped my legs around his waist.

The next moment, we tore each others clothes. We are in his bed competely naked and I'm ridding on him. We are not using protection and we don't care about it because right now we want each other.

"You are so tight.. Fuck", he holds on me tightly. "You feel so good baby", he keeps thrusting me hard and fast. "L-Laszlo I'm gonna cum", I moan loudly. "Cum with me baby", he speeds up.

"Oh god!!", I moan as his mouth dips below and finds my erect nipple. He sucksme and leaves me wanting more.

I felt my walls tighten around him and clench painfully inside me, bringing him to his release with me. I felt his hot semen inside me, trailing down my inner thighs.

"That was.....amazing. You did so good baby", he kissed my forehead. "I agree", I'm in his arms and he lays down in bed holding me. "I will get you pill tomorrow", I laugh at him. "It's okay. I'm a doctor Jason. I will get it tomorrow", he chuckles.

After some time, he gave a home tour, he literally has a theatre in his home. I decided that we would watch movies. He was hesitant at first, but I convinced him.

We are in his theatre. He has recliners and big space. I laid on top of him watching movie. He is stiff, he is really not used to cuddling.

"Relax Laszlo, it's just a movie", I press a kiss on his chest. He relaxed his body. "You don't watch movies?", I draw small patterns on his chest by my fingers.

"No, Arlo comes here with his friends to watch movies or for parties. I don't have friends, I have been all alone in my life", my heart breaks when I hear it.

He doesn't have any friends. My Laszlo spent 29 years all alone. I snuggle more close to him. "You have me now. You're not alone anymore. I kiss his cheek, he plays with my hair and looks at me.

"Do you promise that you'll never leave me?", he questioned me with sad eyes. "I don't think I'll ever leave you. I need you in my life. Do you need me?", I stroke his cheeks.

"Yes, I need you too. I need your body pressed against mine, your warmth, your smell and I need you in my arms everyday baby", he kissed me. I'm so happy, he is everything to me.

The rest of the day we both relax and enjoy time by spending with each other. He cook delicious food for me. I can see a difference in his behaviour, with others he keeps a distance, a serious look on face and doesn't speaks too much.

But with me he laughs, annoys the hell out of me, cooks food for me, make me laugh at his possessiveness and silly jokes. I like it. I like it because he shows this side of him only to me.

Next day, he woke up earlier than me. I get ready for work in front of mirror. I see Jason behind me, he hugs me from behind and rests his chin on my shoulder. I hold his hands.

"When will I see you today? ", he closed his eyes. God, he is really becoming clingy day by day.

"I think we both had spent enough time with each other, you can leave without me for one day at least", I smile looking up through the mirror.

"I'm gonna miss you. Wait.....we will stay here, one more day please", he pouts his lips. "We can't Laszlo. You have tons of work, I need to go to hospital".

"You are not gonna miss me", I turn to face him. "No", I hide my smile. "Ouch. It really hurts baby", he fake crys. I laugh at him and do his tie.

"You can call me, you can visit me when your work is done. I'm not going anywhere", I kiss him and he kisses all over my face.

Later he drops me off, in the hospital. I meet everyone. "Oh god I missed you so much Kira. These both men annoyed the hell out of me", she hugs me tight. "I want to know details of everything after work", I laugh and nod at her.

I get a message from Jason.

LaszloI miss you □

Jesus, he has really become clingy now. I smile at his message. The realization hits me.....

I have fallen for him really hard and fast.

Chapter - 16 - Jealous

J ASON

She's my end. I want to spend my life with her. I knew the second I saw her. She destroyed all the walls I built. She stole my entire heart. I love her. I love her so much, and I'm happy about it.

I hope she feels the same for me. Even if she doesn't love me, I will fight for her. I will wait for her, but I'm never letting her go. I will not let my past destroy my present. It's better if I don't tell her anything.

I trust her, I'm gonna tell her how I feel about her. I'm scared that she will reject me. I have become fucking addicted to her.

My office door opens and Arlo comes in. He is on wheel chair. He got discharged from hospital, but still his leg is fractured. He has a caretaker with him. Of course, I appointed a old lady for him.

"It's good to see you brother, so how was your vacation", he winks at me. "It was perfect. I enjoyed it", I don't look at him.

"So....was she good? I bet she_____"."Arlo, respect her. This your last warning", I gave my serious look.

"Chill bro. By the way, mama is dying to see her"."What? Why would you tell her. I was going to introduce her", I run my hand through my hair.

"You know her. She knows that you don't take holidays or go for vacations, and when it comes to her favorite son, that is you.... she doesn't back down", he explains himself. It's true, we can't hide anything from mama.

"I will talk to her. Kira needs time to adjust. I don't want to stress her out ", I said. "Aww, look at you. Who would have thought you have this side too. A soft, possessive boyfriend", he mocks me and laugh.

"Enough about me. What about you? Why are you here?", he only meets me when he wants something. "Yes. I...I...I mean if you are going to meet Kira today, I'll accompany you". Oh no way!!!

"Why? Arlo I swear if_____"."Relax. I want to accompany, because I...I like a guy...and he's kinda friend of Kira. So.. ", he is nervous. I know this look.

"Oh... So you have a crush on him. Julius right?"."Yes, he's the guy", he blushed. Payback time bitch. "I will tell him that my lil brother is having a crush on you", I mock him. He is shocked because I never behave like this. Our conversation always used to be short.

"You wouldn't do that. Hell, what's wrong with you", he's annoyed and I laugh at him. "God, she has really changed you. I like this side of you", he chuckles.

"I.... I love her. She is...is really special to me. I still didn't tell her that but I'm planning to tell her", I'm literally blushing.

"You fucking asshole. I'm so happy for you. If I was not in this fucking wheel chair I would have hugged you so bad, but you don't like hugs. It's okay", he cheers.

I went close to him and lean down and hugged him. He was surprised. "You never hugged me willingly bro", he hugged me back tight.

"Don't do anything stupid. Kira is my friend too", he said. "Is this a warning? ", I chuckle. "Yes, the one you should take seriously", I hit him and he winced in pain.

I will finish the work as soon possible and I'll meet her. I messaged her, she was literally pissed off. What's my fault, I only messages her 26th time today.

It was late evening, Arlo comes with me. We wait for them down at the receptionist. My eyes are searching for her. I spotted her with her friends, but also with a new guy. Who the hell is he, and why is he is standing so close to her?

"Look at your face, you look so funny when you're jealous", Arlo laughs at me. "Shut up Arlo".

She looks at me and walk towards me with her friends. Why is he coming with her? God, I want to punch his face for no reason. When they are close enough the guy is shocked. Of course he knows who I am.

She comes and hugs me and I hug her tight. She whispers in my ear, "Babe, you look stressed", she whispers in my ear and I calm down instantly. She knows me so well.

I snuggled my head in her neck. I don't care about anyone. "Laszlo, everyone is watching at us", she said but I kept her close to me.

I greet all her friends and here is the guy. "Laszlo, he is my friend Lance. Lance, he is my boyfriend Jason", she introduced him.

"Fuck, you are dating Jason Knight", yes fucker, is he deaf? "We should leave now", I look at her and she nods. "Kira, we will discuss the next surgery tomorrow". Oh hell no!!! I glare at him and he is already scared of me.

"Ok guys let's go to some restaurant", Maximus said. "No, Lasz____"."I would love to", I interrupted her and she is surprised. "Great come on", April said.

Kira comes near me, "You don't have to do that"."No, it's fine. Your friends are important to you in your life and I don't want to take that away from you", I was going to kiss her...

"Hey, you guys coming", Lance interrupted us. Motherfucker, why is he coming with us. I hope I can control my anger. I don't want Kira to be scared of me.

Arlo is near me, "I know you are jealous, he is already scared of you, leave the poor guy alone", he said. "I'm not jealous of that guy and shut the fuck up", I whisper it to him.

We go to a restaurant near by. Their are only quite few people here, so no will know about me. We all get seated. Kira sits next to me, but the Lance guy is sitting next to us. He is staring at my baby. God, I really want to pluck his eyeballs out.

Everyone is chatting, laughing and pulling each others leg. Kira is enjoying it, she is laughing. Her laugh brings a smile to ky face. My eyes don't leave her, even for a second. She caught me staring, but I don't care about it.

"Stop staring at me", she whispers and smiles at me. "Come home with me. Please don't put a fight", I gave her my sad face.... I hope it works.

"Ok Laszlo", she kissed my nose. Yes, it worked. I kiss her forehead and her lips. I did it purposely to show Lance who she belonged to.

We get interrupted again by a woman. She sits beside Lance. "Lance, why are you here with_____", she looks at me and stops. She is shocked, her mouth is wide open.

"Oh my god!!!Jason Knight and Arlo Knight are sitting in front of me. I really wanted to meet you both at the hospital but I couldn't. Hii, I'm Amy Duncan. I also work at the hospital".She is chatter box. She is talking non stop.

I don't even know what this woman is talking about. "Amy, just fucking stop. Give yourself a break", thank god April shouts at her. Great, just fucking great. I'm pissed off because of the fucker Lance, and now this woman. Her voice is so annoying.

"Ignore her. Anyways, you know my father, he is a committee member of hospital. I would like you invite your family to dinner", she winks at me. I don't know how Arlo is isn't flirting with her.

"I don't know you. I don't trust people and I don't trust you", everyone starts laughing, and she looks pissed. "My father is Robert Duncan", my food is getting cold so I was busy eating. I didn't paid attention to her. Everyone try to hide their smiles.

"Jason I was thinking_____"."Stop. First of all don't call me with my name. Let me tell you one thing, I don't like women throwing themselves at me. I don't care whose daughter you are, so stop trying", I gave her my best warning face.

"Baby, if you are finished, we shall leave", I hold her hand, she nods her head. We are about to leave I heard Amy saying, "Worthless slut, always fucking sleeping with men", and I stop.

"What did you fucking said", I shout and my voice is clearly audible to everyone. "N- No, I..I..didn't say a-anything", she was lying. I was about to go near her, but Kira stopped me. "Laszlo, let's leave", she holds my hand. "How could she say that to you", I was so angry.

"She didn't said anything, will you stop overreacting", Lance said and I glare at him. He looks scared as shit. "I-I mean s-she...", he couldn't even able to complete because,I grab his shirt collar.

Arlo comes and tries to apart us, but I don't leave him. "Laszlo please....". I look at her, she is scared. I leave his collar. She holds my hand, we leave the restaurant. We don't say a word to each other, the whole drive. We reached my home, why isn't she saying something? We are in my bedroom.

"Baby, I___",she hugs me tight and I wrap my arms around her. "I'm sorry, I didn't mean to shout, but I can't tolerate, if someone says bad about you", I dip my head in her neck. "It's my fault. I should have not agreed to the dinner in the first place. It's okay", she whispers in my ear.

"No, it's not you. I'll try not to do that again", why is she apologizing, it's my fault. I kiss her forehead.

"Kira, I...I... ", why can't I say it.

Chapter - 17 - Who hurt him?

K IRA

Warning This chapter contains mature scenes.

"Kira I..I.....".."Yes", I stroke his cheek. He looks so handsome, he leans down my hand.

"I think you should rest now", he said. Why is he so nervous today? "Are you sure nothing is bothering you", I'm really worried about him.

"Yes Kira. You should rest now", he kissed my forehead. After some time we both lay down on bed. I'm in his arms while he is playing with my hair. I recall what happened few moments ago.

I knew Jason was uncomfortable because of Lance's presence. And when Amy arrived, I also knew she would flirt with him. Amy had said several things about me, she even spread fake rumours, but I didn't paid any attention to her.

Because I already had enough on my plate, and Amy is isn't worthy of my time. I laugh how he was jealous the whole dinner.

"Why are you laughing?", he smiles at me. I look up at him. "Just recalling the moment when you were jealous. You should have seen your face", I started laughing hard.

"Baby stop. I don't want to remember that", I giggled. I squeezed his both cheeks in my hands, "Aww....you look cute when you're jealous".

"I admit it. I was jealous. I get jealous when someone else has your attention. It's not even because I'm needy or insecure. I just don't want someone else to realize how amazing you are...and for them to steal you away from me. I just...really don't want to lose you. You mean so much to me for that to happen", he kissed my forehead and closed his eyes.

Wow...I can't believe he said that. "Mister, you better open your eyes. I can't believe after saying sweet things to me you are sleeping now!!!", I hit his chest and he chuckles.

"Why, do I turn you on? Answer me baby", he sucks my earlobe in his mouth. "Y-Yes", I whisper. "Good, I'm not planning to go slow tonight", he kissed me hard.

I was on top of him. I started removing his pants, he was already hard for me. "Look at me. This is how you make me hard", he moans out. I wanted to pleasure him, so I grab his hard long cock in my hand slowly. My hand is small around his penis. I started moving my hand you and down around his hard cock.

He throws his head back and moans, "Fuck...", I smile looking at him. I want to tease him a bit. I started with long, slow licks from top to bottom, then teased a little with my tongue on the tip.

"Baby please...stop teasing me", he groans and cover his face with his hand. I lick the precum off the head. I took his cock into my mouth and started sucking him. He moans again, I love hearing him moan. I feel him grow as he becomes more excited.

"Fuck...keep doing that, you are doing so good Kira", he moans my name. He grabs a fistful of my hair in his hand and controls me. He is really long. I try my best to take it whole in my mouth. I don't stop. I picked up the pace, I started to suck hard and fast.

"K-Kira...I don't think I can hold anymore", I started deepthroathing him. "Fuck Kira, I'm gonna cum", he looks at me. I deepthroat him nonstop and finally he moans my name louder, "KIRAAA....", I feel his rope of cum in my mouth and I swallowed it.

I look at him, he is still semi hard. How is he still hard. He grabs me and switched positions. He is now on top of me. "My turn baby", he took my panties off. I'm completely naked. "You are always ready for me.You are so wet baby", he sucks my neck.

Without any warning he thrusts inside me, I moan. "Ohh..God", he gives me a minute to adjust his size. After knowing that I'm comfortable he thrusts me hard and fast. He really doesn't show mercy on me. He bites my neck, sucks my nipples but does not stop fucking me. He is constantly hitting my G-spot, he throws my one leg on his shoulder and fucks me hard.

"J-Jason I....".""I know baby, cum with me", he whispers in my ear. He shoots another load of cum inside me. We can hear each other's breathing. He rests his face in my neck. I can't feel my legs.

"Another round?".Fuck, doesn't he get tired. I guess we are going for a another round.

————————————

"Aren't you gonna be late for hospital?"."Yes I am. Thanks to you, I can barely walk", I give him a sarcastic smile. "Welcome baby", he kissed my forehead and laughs.

It's been months now. We started staying at each others homes every night. Not even a single night we are apart from each other. I don't know what he sees in me. He takes care of me and he is also very possessive of me.

He is sweet, loving and caring boyfriend. But I know there's something more. I can see the pain in his eyes, and I was fully sure when I got to know he has nightmares. Even during our vacation he got nightmares and also till today.

I still remember some nights when he had a nightmare.

FLASHBACK

It was midnight. I felt something moving under me. I opened my eyes I saw Jason, he was trembling in fear. I heard everything that he said.

"Please....I-I'm s-sorry, I won't do it again. I-It hurts", I can see tears on his cheeks.

"No....don't call them. T-They will h-hurt me again. I-I-It pains a lot", hearing everything he said, it broke my heart. Who would have hurt him? I don't know why, but I want to take his pain away. I can't see him like this.

"Shh...Laszlo it's me. Calm down, I'm here", I whisper in his ear and he calms down. I pull him over me. His head is on my chest, I stroke my fingers in his hair. He tightens his hold around me.

"Hey...it's okay. I'm here now, calm down baby", I said and kissed his forehead and wiped his tears.

FLASHBACK OVER.

This happens some nights. He holds me tight, he sweats, I see tears run down his closed eyes that always break my heart. Because I can't do anything. He talks in his sleep, his breathing quickens, but I immediately hold him and he calms down.

When I mentioned him before, he was really uncomfortable and nervous. I don't want to force him in any situation. I'm still waiting for him to open up for me, and when he does, I will do anything to take his pain away.

He called me and said to come to his home. He was excited to tell me that he has something planned for me, it's a surprise.

I was happy to hear this. I finished all my work, he sent Liam to pick me up. Liam is Jason's bodyguard. I would say he's more than a bodyguard to him. Liam is best friend of Jason since they were kids. He is good and kind.

I go upstairs to his room. I opened the door, but he's nowhere. I thought he might be in kitchen. I was about to leave I spot him in the corner of the room.

He wrapped himself and his head is in his knees. I noticed his right hand was bleeding badly. Fuck. I ran towards him, I sit down on my knees.

"Laszlo w-what happened?".

Chapter - 18 - I lost her

JASON

It's been months, we have been together. We couldn't leave apart from each other. I was so fucking addicted to her. She is like a light to my darkness, and I will never let her go.

I know she is helping me with my nightmares, because it's not that painful anymore. I don't even remember because, she holds me every night. She understands me, she also is my comfort zone.

From the moment she came to my life, she changed everything. I like this new change. I don't think, I can hide it anymore from her, that I love her. I love her so much.

I'm proposing her tonight. I don't care what her answer will be, but I want her to know that she's my whole heart. I can do anything for her.

I called her and said to come home, and I sent Liam to pick her up. Before she will be there, I went to florist shop to buy flowers, she loves flowers. I plan a romantic dinner.

I gave order this evening itself. I ordered her favorite dishes. I never did this before, so I don't have any experience in this. I want to do it all by myself for her. I bought flowers and I'm currently in the hotel to pick up the order.

Fuck, I'm so nervous but I'm excited too. I want to go further on this new chapter with her. Someone taps my shoulder from behind and I turned myself, I couldn't believe my eyes.

"Hey man, are you finished? I want to give my order next", I didn't expected to see him again. I thought h-he was....No, not again. My face is covered with sweat.

"Are you okay", he asked again. I immediately run from the hotel. I don't want to see his face. I hate his cruel voice. After so many years, why is he here? Does he know about me?

No, I cannot let this happen again. I was finally forgetting him, I wanted to forget my past with him, but he showed up. My legs are shaking in fear. My heart is pounding right out of chest.

Why him? I found my way to my car. "Take me home now!!!", I said to my driver. I constantly turn back, it feels like he's following me. "Are you okay sir", my driver asks me. I just nod at him. I couldn't even speak.

I'm feeling weak. I'm grown ass man now, but still I'm trembling in fear. He makes me feel weak. I can't believe his back again. My whole body is shaking.

I reached home. I run towards my room. I don't want anyone to see me like this. As I enter my room, I walk to bathroom. I splash cold water on my face. I see myself in mirror. I look at myself, how weak I am.

How can this happen. Seeing his face face brings all my memories back. Tears come out of my eyes. I covered up my scars, but it's still visible to me. It's like I can see all my scars. I can feel them on my body.

I rub my chest, my hands, everywhere. I want to get rid of this feeling but I can't. I'm angry. I'm angry on myself. Why is this happening to me again? Why I can't rid of this pain? I remember everything. Every word and every memory.

FLASHBACK

I was like a slave to him. He used to abuse me everydayHe used to give me sometime to heal, and again hit me everyday. The same procedure everyday. I even wanted to die sometimes, rather than living with him.

He grabbed my jaw in his fingers harshly, "You are nothing. You are just weak and pathetic", he slaps my face. "Go cook some dinner for me and remember if it tastes bad, I will break you fucking hand. You are nothing but weak".

FLASHBACK OVER.

His words ring in my head. I cover my ears withy both hands, still his voice is audible to me.

"No, I'm not weak!!!", I shout at myself. I break the mirror in front of me with my bare hand. My knuckles is covered with blood. This doesn't pain a lot, I have suffered much worse than this.

I'm not in my right mind. I don't know what's going on with me. I don't understand what's real. Images are playing in front of me. I sit in corner of my room. I want to be alone for some time.

I wrap my hands around myself. I'm going insane. I need to be alone or I might hurt someone, so I hide myself in the corner of my room.

I rock myself back and forth in the corner. I hear someone opened the door and I stop. Did he followed me to my home? I hope he doesn't see me. I get all the images in front of me, were he hurt me. I don't even look who is it.

I sense someone in front of me. I was scared to death. I couldn't even hear the voice, who is next to me. Without even thinking for once, I grab the neck of the next person with my other hand. All I can see is his face. I grab it tightly, he was struggling.

"I'm not weak anymore. Y-You can't hurt me", My grip on his neck tightens more and more. I can see him struggling to breathe.

"J-Jason...leave me. Y-You're h-hurting me", he deserves all the pain, that he has caused me.

"L-Laszlo ple-please", he never called me with my middle name. It suddenly hits me, there is only one person who calls me with my middle name. I immediately move back and I shake my head, trying to come into my senses.

I see Kira, she's on the floor...trying to catch her breathe. No no no, what I've done. I hurt her. I imagined that she was____Shit, I go near her and try to help her, but she moves back.

I can see tears in her eyes. Her eyes showed pure fear. She is scared of me. I fucked up everything in just minutes. "K-Kira, I....", "No, ple-please don't c-come near m-me", It broke my heart. I just did something, that her abusive ex did to her. She gets up and runs away for me.

Tears are not stopping coming out of my eyes. I just fucked up bad. I committed a very big mistake. I pull my hair. I'm angry on myself so much. I try to go after her but she's nowhere to be found. God, where did she go?

I called Liam, "Liam, try to find Kira, s-she just left now. I-I couldn't able to find her", I'm so scared. "Jason what you did?", I just fucked up everything. "Liam, try to find her please. Don't end the call", I'm so worried about her.

"I can see her, she's walking on street alone", THANK GOD. "Just drop her home safely, and call me later", I end the call.

I just lost her. How am I gonna fix this? Why, he had to show up now? I sit down on floor near my bed. I didn't wanted to spend my evening like this. I should've called her right after I saw him.

I slap myself, I look down my handsHow did I hurt her? How did I hurt my baby? She's never gonna forgive me. I realized that whatever I do or try to be, atlast there is gonna be the same result. That is, I'm not worthy of her. I never was and I don't think I'll ever be.

Chapter-19-You are not my Laszlo..

K^{IRA}

It happened again. The thing I was most afraid of, happened again with me. I got hurt again, but from different person. The person I trusted the most, he just chocked me to death.

The incident that happened, is playing before me continuously. I don't think I will forget his angry face. His cruel and heartless emotions. My neck is still paining, but not more than the pain that is caused to my heart.

I trusted him. I...I love him. Why he would do that to me? Knowing that it will pain me more. It showed that he never cared about me. I was begging him to let go, but he didn't listened.

I'm now in middle of street. My eyes are covered in tears. I ran as fast as I can. I don't want to see him ever again. It's all my fault. I should've not trusted him...and I got my prize.

I hear someone calling my name. I think it might be Jason. I don't want to see him. I was so afraid. "Kira stop. Kira, it's me Liam", I hear him. I turn myself around. He looks at me and gets worried. "Kira are yo___", I didn't even let him complete the sentence. I stop him. "Liam please l-leave me alone. P-please", a tear ran down my cheek.

He comes near me, "No, it's not safe. I will drop you, come".I'm in the car with him. I don't say a word to him, but he breaks the silence. "I know, it's not my business, but what happened between you two?", he looks at me. I was sitting beside him.

"I don't want to t-talk about i-it", It hurts a lot while speaking. "I just wanted to say that Jason is a difficult person to be around. But he's really a good guy", ofcourse no one knows him.

"Y-Yeah, even he c-chokes you to death. H-He is r-really a good p-person", I shrug. Liam is shocked, as he heard me. He looks at me and saw the marks on my neck. "Fuck Kira, I didn't knew__", I cut him again. "Of course, you didn't know. J-Just drop m-me h-home", I don't look at him.

"Kira, he has suffered a lot in past. I know what he did to you is totally wrong, but give him some time, he___"."No, I-I can't....I'm tired L-Liam. I-I don't think I c-can give him time. He doesn't h-have fucking balls to tell me about his p-past, but he c-can choke me, RIGHT!!!", I shout out loudly.

"I don't want to talk about this a-anymore", I was angry, but I was more sad. Why him? After all these years, I finally love someone, who is my whole heart. But when I saw his face back there....he was not my Laszlo, that I love. He was a monster.

I reached my apartment. I took out my scarf and wrap it around my neck. I don't want anyone to know about it. "Hey, Jason is not here with you?", Arlo asked me. He is actually living with us because of Julius. They both are in a relationship and totally in love with each other. "He h-has some work, he w-won't be coming tonight", I don't look at him. "Are you fine?"."Yes

A-Arlo. I'm j-just tired", I cover the scarf more so that he won't see. I rush in my roomI lock the door. I could not stop crying. I check my phone. Jason is calling me continuously. He is messaging too. I don't want to hear his harsh voice. I don't think I will be able to face him anymore.

Next morning, the pain is even worse. I wore some oversized shirt to cover up my neck. I switch off my phone. I don't want him to contact me.

I'm currently in my office checking out some files. Even after what he did to me, I still miss him. Why? I try to distract myself and keep myself busy with some files. Suddenly my office door opens and I see him...

"Kira______", "Why are y-you here?", I cut him in middle. "I'm worried about you. I'm sorry Kira I shouldn't have done that to you", I couldn't stop myself from crying in front of him. I look like a idiot.

"No, baby please don't cry I___", "Stop calling m-me that. I don't want you h-here. Just l-leave me a-alone", I get up from my chair. "L-Leave Mr. Knight", I show my hand at the door. "Laszlo..call me Laszlo", the fucking nerve of him.

"No, you are n-not my Laszlo I-I know.P-Please leave"."I can't leave", he comes near me. I take a step back. "Please Kira", he tries to catch my hand. "Don't you d-dare fucking t-touch me. Get out of m-my office", I shout at him.

His face falls down. He looked hurt, but I don't care. Last night incident plays in my front of me. I turn myself, my back is faced to him.

"I love you Kira", a tear runs down my cheek. I was craving those three words from him so much. Oh...Laszlo why would do this to me. After hearing those words, I just feel sad. If last night incident wouldn't hap-pened, I would've been so happy. I would've also told him that I love him so much. Everything changed, in just one night.

All I feel is anger. I turn to him, "Stop saying t-that....you d-don't. If you d-did you wouldn't have done t-that", he doesn't look at me. "It was only m-me right. I was t-the only o-one that trusted you. I was t-the only one t-that loved you. You didn't", I let out a small laugh.

"I should've listened what the world says about you. You are the most selfish, cruel, self-centered and heartless man. You d-don't love anything. Y-You didn't even t-trusted me with your past. And here I was.... I shared my past with y-you", I let out a small laugh. "So stupid o-of me, ri___", I wasn't able to complete the sentence, because I was coughing badly.

"Kira calm down please just_____", "What do y-you want from m-me now!!! You wanted to fuck me, and congratulations...you did. Mission accomplished. Now go find someone e-else to statisfy y-your needs!!!", I saw tears on his cheeks, that broke my heart. But I have a emotionless expression on my face.

He wipes his tears and looks at me, "You don't want to listen to me...Fine. I know you need some time, and I will give you that. I'm sorry for what I did. I'm ashamed of myself too. But listen carefully....You are mine, and you will always be mine.I will fight for you. I will fight for you, until you forgive me. Take care Kira", he says and leaves the office.

I can't believe him. After everything he did, he thinks I will be with him. I see Liam in front of me. He gives me a small napkin to wipe my tears.

"Thanks Liam. Y-You should g-go", I continue to do my work. "Ahh....act ually I can't", he takes a seat in front of me. "Why?", I have a confused look on my face.

"Well....Jason appointed me as your personal bodyguard, to take care of you"."What!!! I don't need anyone and tell him to not interfere in my life", I was so angry on Jason. "See, if I go back, he will not hesitate to kill me.

You want me to be killed..", he fake cries. I cover my my face with my hands. God, why is he doing this to me.

I see Liam having a huge smile on his face. "God, I hate both of you. Are you gonna follow me everywhere now", I asked in disbelief. "Yes ma'am. Your safety is my top priority", I hit his shoulder and he laughs.

I don't understand why Jason is doing this. There is no point in this. He was serious about the bodyguard thing. He was literally following me everywhere. I hate Jason so much right now.

Lance came near me, for discussing some case papers."Hey dude, if you don't want any broken bones in your body, I suggest you to maintain some distance", I can't believe him. I look at him in disbelief. "I'll.....meet you....l-later",he and leaves.

"Seriously!!!Liam I think it's too much", he shrugs. "These are orders from my boss. I need to follow them".. He doesn't have have right to do this.

"You know what, Fuck you and your boss", I shout and leave.

He messed up everything, and he is trying to do it worse. I don't plan to see him anymore now.

Chapter - 20 - Disappointed..

Jason

I deserve it. I deserve everything that she said.... But my heart broke when she said that I was using her. I would never do that to her. I didn't slept that night. How would I? When I lost my baby.

I'm all alone again. Arlo is angry with me because he knows what happened between us. I remember, how he came last night...

I was in my room, sitting in the corner. I hear my door open again. I got up, I thought Kira came back. But it was Arlo. He was angry, and by his looks I know...he knows everything.

"A-Arlo, have you______", I wasn't able to finish, I felt a sharp pain on my left cheek. I realized that he punched me. I deserve it. He grabbed my shirt collar. I didn't stopped him.

"How could you do that? How could you hurt her, you fucking asshole", he punched me again. "I don't care you are my brother right now. I warned you...How could you that to the woman you love?", I couldn't able to look at him. He was so mad at me.

He didn't leave my collar, " Why would you hurt Kira. Hell, you know how it feels to get abused. I didn't expected this from you", he said in disgust.

"Stop it Arlo. Leave him", I look up and I see Liam. He tries to apart us. "You know what he did to her?", Arlo asked Liam, and he just nods. "Arlo, I can understand it. I'm controlling myself too. I want to beat up his face, but I know him, we should listen to his side of story. I swear if he is wrong in anyway, I won't stop you", Arlo wasn't interested in anyway.

"Would you speak up now asshole?", Arlo was trying to control his anger. Liam gives me a understanding nod, to speak up. "I-I....saw him...", I told them everything that happened, they couldn't believe what I said.

"No....this can't happen. H-He's dead. I don't u-understand....the cops told us that___", Arlo didn't believe me. "I know Arlo!!But, I saw him", I was shaking in pure fear. "Are you sure Jason? You must have_____", "Liam, trust me, I did and I'm hundred percent sure", my legs don't support me anymore. I take the support of the wall.

Liam comes to help me. He's always there for me. Every fucking time, but I never appreciated him. After, what happened with me, I build up a wall and shut everyone. But he was always there for me.

"Liam, I didn't wanted to hurt her. I didn't....I-I was n-not in my right m-mindset. I-I just snapped", I was crying. I don't care what they think of me.

Arlo came near me and hugged me. "I'm sorry for what happened, but I'm not sorry for punching you", he looks at me and I know he's still pissed off.

"You should've told her. Why were you hiding it from her?", he asked me. "I thought she would leave me. Who would be still with me, even after knowing the truth", Arlo shakes his head in disbelief.

"You love her, that means you take care of her, be with her and most important you trust her. You didn't trust her with your past, but she did. She did everything with you and what you gave her in return, huh!!! I won't forgive you for this. You know what... after everything you did she didn't even said anything to anyone...She left you, because you were not a man enough to trust her. You made a mistake, so you are gonna fix this", he says and leaves.

He stops in middle and turns, "But if you hurt her in the process...I won't hesitate to throw punches on you again", he leaves. "I'm gonna investigate on this. Don't worry about him but Kira. You need to win her back man... and clean your hand...it's covered in blood", I hug him. He was surprised but he hugs me back.

"Thanks for being there with me"."Hey, you are my best friend and I'm your bodyguard too. I will always be your side and protect you", he smiles.

––––––––––––––––––––

How I'm gonna fix this? I told her that she can take her time but I can't. How am I gonna be without her. Just not being with her for one day, made me this miserable. Next few days are gonna to more painful.

––––––––––––––––––––

I don't want to stay in my room. Whenever I ever enter my room. I remember what I did to her. Without her it feels empty. I can't stay here. I need someone to talk about it. And there's only one person who would hear me out.

I don't think about anything, I just drive my car. I reached up to my destination. I enter the house, "Oh my god!! How are you? Why you didn't call me for so many days? I'm so happy to see you", she hugs me tightly.

"Mama, breathe. I'm good. How have you been?", she hugs me tight in response. "Mama, I need to talk to you", she examines my face and nods. As the moment we enter her room and she sat down on bed... I lay my head on her lap. She runs her hand through my hair.

"Jason, you are scaring me. Talk to me", I sit up and I look at her. "Mama, I really hurt her so bad. I don't know what to do?", I was crying again. "Jason, I don't understand anything. Tell me from beginning", she wipes away my tears.

I told her everything. By the looks of her, I know that she was disappointed in me. "I don't want to talk about that man, and I really think you have mistaken it__"."No mama___", "Let me complete. But it's not fair for Kira. I know you didn't wanted to hurt her, but eventually you did. She don't deserve this. I never thought you would do this. I'm so disappointed in you", she doesn't look at me.

"Mama, I know I committed a very big mistake. Please help me to make it right", she looks at me and takes a deep breathe. "Jason, first of all you give her the time she needs. After that....show her how much you love her. No matter how many days or months it may take...you will try to win her back. We are 'Knights' we don't give up without trying. But remember you won't force her in anyway", she gives me a sad smile.

"And most important...you need to clear the misunderstanding between you two....and the only way is that you need to tell her the truth is...about your past", she sighs.

"And yes, I want to meet her. So you better fix this before you are too late. You will not call me till then and remember I will only see you if you are with Kira", she just leaves me alone in the room. It's not going to be easy.

———————————————

Weeks went by, everyday I send her flowers and a note with it. I call her but she doesn't pick up. I message her, but she doesn't read it too. She's giving me the cold shoulder. I'm craving to listen her sweet voice.

I watch her secretly from my car at long distance. I appointed Liam, to be with her. I watch her, she's not like herself. I want to hug her, keep her in my arms and bring a smile to her face. But I can't. I hate this so much.

I don't live at my house. I live with my family. Mama is still pissed off with me. It's 6:00 pm now. I spend my evening in the park. I sit down on one of the benches. I come here everyday in this park. I watch other people with their families. I watch how happy they are.

I feel a gentle tap on my shoulder. I see a small girl sitting beside me. She's really beautiful with a cute ponytail and she is having a stuff bear in her hands. She is smiling at me. "Are you okay Mister?", Is she talking to me, I look behind me, but there is no one. She giggled. "I'm talk to you", she pats my thigh. I smile hearing her cute english.

"Y-Yeah, I-I'm fine. Why did you asked?", she was atleast five year old. I look around me, but I don't see her parents. "I see you everyday, you look sad", she just stares at me. What should I say?

"Why are you sad?", she questions me again. "Umm-I__I hurt someone really bad and she kinda....left me", god why am I speaking to her. She's just a kid. I look at her, she's already confused. "Do you want to hug my teddy bear. He loves hug", she stretches out her stuff toy in front of me.

I just smile at her and close my eyes. I feel a warm presence around me. I opened my eyes, I was surprised to see her, she was hugging me. Her small hands were wrapped around my neck. My hands automatically wrap her. After so many days someone was hugging me. She reminded me a lot like my Kira.

"Thank you so much Angel", she giggled again. "My name is Ella", she smiles at me. If this little girl would have met me months ago, I would have probably shouted at her or even scared her off. "You are just like my teddy bear who loves hugs", I laugh with her. She totally changed my mood.

I notice some red lines on her shoulder. "Did you get hurt?", I am concerned for her. "I-I.... I fell in park", she smiles at me. "You should go now. Your parents must be worried about you Angel", her face falls down but she nods.

She gets up with her teddy bear in her hands and walks away. She doesn't even look at me, but she stops and takes a glance at me. She comes running back to me and kissed my cheek. "Bye, Mr. Teddy bear", she giggles. "Bye Angel".

I get a call from Liam, "Hey Jason, I don't know how to say this, Kira and her friends are in the club right now. She is not ready to listen to me.. I think you should come here", why is he so nervous. "Liam send me your location, I will be there, don't allow anyone to come near her", god this woman will be death of me.

Chapter - 21 - Second Chance?

K IRA

It's been weeks now. He gave me the time I needed. I miss him so much. I feel empty without him. He is sending me flowers everyday, with a message on it. There a knock on the door, "Kira, it's definitely for you", April shouts.

I open, it's not a surprise. I see a bouquet of flowers, but this was much more bigger than the others and with a message. "What happened between both of you? Is it serious", April asked me. "Yeah something like that", I don't look at her. "Hey, I don't know what happened between both of you....but I think you should atleast give him a chance to explain himself", she hands me a cup of coffee.

I donate those flowers, but I keep the letters. I remember every message that was written. I read today's message, "I'm sorry baby. Please give me a chance to explain myself. Just give me 15 minutes...I promise I won't bother you anymore", I thought that he would forget about me and move on. But he's not giving up, that makes me feel happy.

I don't know how I am going to forgive him. I really miss him so much. "Seriously Kira, if you're so called personal bodyguard is staying with us everyday.....then he will also pay the rent with us", April came shouting at me, with Liam behind her.

"Liam, what do you need now? It's my day off, I'm not working today", Liam didn't even leave my side. He is also staying at night in the living room. I don't understand why is he following Jason order so seriously?

"Missed me, I know you did", he winks at April. He annoys the hell out of her. "I'm going to the roof top, you both can continue", I say and leave. I go to the terrace. I sit on the platform and watch the sky. I remember the moments with Jason, it brings a smile to my face.

"You miss him?", Liam sits beside me and watch the view with me. "Yes.. ..it's just that....everything between us is so messy right now, I don't know how to fix this", I sigh. "Kira I can't see him like that. He rarely goes for work, he is staying with his family....but his mama said he doesn't come out if his room. He is miserable without you", he doesn't look at me.

"I know. He is always in my mind. I tried to forget him Liam, but I couldn't. I feel bad for what he did to me, but I feel more pain that he couldn't trust me enough. But still here I am missing him so much. I even miss his stupid forehead kisses", a sob escaped from my mouth.

"He realised his mistake now. Give him a chance to explain himself. Because I don't want to go to the damn hospital everyday, I hate that smell and I want to sleep in my house and on my bed", he said in one breathe and I laugh at him.After so many days, I laughed.

"Thanks Liam, for everything. You really helped me in these days. You are really a good friend. Thank you", I hug him and he hugs me back.

My phone rang in my pocket. I pick it up, "Kira, we are going to the club and you're coming with us", she doesn't even allow me to say anything.

I look up at Liam, "I guess we are going to club Liam. I need to distract myself".

"Umm... I...don't think that's a good idea", Liam said nervously. "It's okay Liam, we are just gonna have some drinks", he just nods.

———————————

We reached the club. I don't remember when was the last time I came to club. April got drinks for us. Arlo and Julius were busy kissing each other and well Maximus is busy flirting with women.

I swear I decided to drink only few drinks, but I ended up drinking more. I think I know the reason....Jason. God, even after drinking alcohol, I'm not able to forget him.

"Hey beautiful, do you wanna dance", I look up... I see a handsome man standing in front of me. But he is not as handsome as Jason. "Sure", I stood up, but Liam stopped me, "Kira, he is a stranger. Don't do this", god what is wrong with him.

"Liam, I'm just gonna have some fun. I just want to be happy for sometime. Don't you want that", I pout at him. "B-But Kira Ja____", he was stopped in middle by the man. "Hey dude, she doesn't have any problem. Do you mind", he takes my hand and we hit the dance floor.

I started to dance with him. Even I'm completely dancing with a stranger all I see Jason.Suddenly the man started touching me inappropriately. I only agreed to dance with him, not to hook up with him. I was going to stop him, but I felt a huge presence behind me.

Suddenly, my heart started beating fast. He can't be here right now. I gather all my courage to turn around myself. There he is, am I dreaming?

"Good to see you Kira. Are you having fun?", he was angry. I saw his fist and jaw clenching. Why is he angry? I'm the one who should be angry with him.

"Yeah, I'm having fun. Now, will you mind your own business", now he is really angry with me. "Oh I will Kira, when I'm done with this guy and later with you", I don't know why, but I think he just gave me a warning. "You can't just control my life Jason", I scold him, but he doesn't pay attention to me.

"Remove your filthy hands from her", he said in a demanding voice. The guy was really drunk and he didn't listen to what Jason said.

One thing led to another, they were laying punches to each other. Everyone stopped dancing and got scared. Jason was beating the poor guy continuously and he was bleeding badly. I tried to stop him, "Jason please stop it", but he didn't stop.

But thank god Liam and Arlo came to stop Jason. His hand is bruised badly and with blood. He was breathing heavily and his eyes were on me. I couldn't believe him, he created a scene in front of everyone. I walk out of the club with my purse. "Kira, please stop", I hear Jason calling out my name but I don't stop and I keep walking.

"Kira please listen to me", he grabs my arm to stop me. "What do you want now. Isn't that enough what you did before", I try to move out from his hold. I look at his knuckles that were badly hurt and filled with blood. I instantly stopped and took his hands in mine. "Why do you always keep doing this", I look up at him and saw tears in his eyes.

I take a moment to look up at him. His hair were always used to in perfect way but now they are grown and messy. He has bags under his eyes, clearly stating that he is not having sleep. His eyes are red and swollen. He cried. I didn't knew he would be this miserable without me.

Automatically my hand came up to his cheek. I wanted to run my hand through his hair and say sweet words to him and his head on my chest and my arms around his body.

But I couldn't. He leans down to my hand. "Please Kira, let me explain everything. I will just need 15 minutes. Just listen me out, after that whatever your decision maybe, I will respect that", he pleaded to me. I really wanted to know, why would he do that to me.

I know he is guilty and he is suffering too. Whatever his reason was, but I wanted to give him a second chance. Call me stupid, idiot or lovesick but this is the truth. I was miserable without him too. But I do my best to not show any emotions on my face.

"Okay, Now start speaking", I wait for him to speak. He looks around and looks at me. "Can we go to my house. I don't want this conversation to be in middle of the street", he said. "Jason, I don't think that's a good idea", I don't look at him. Did he really thought I will go with him to his house again.

"It's okay. We can go to your home. I don't want you to feel uncomfortable", he said in a nervous tone. "Let's go then", I said and then we took a cab. In cab we both maintained a distance. April called me and asked me if I was alright. I told her I was heading home with Jason and not to worry about me.

It was such a different feeling. We are currently in the living room. He was clearly confused and nervous. He didn't know how to start the conversation. I break the silence, "I will get some water for you", I head to kitchen. I took a glass of water and turn myself from the kitchen counter Suddenly Jason was in front of me. He took the glass of water from my hand and drank the whole glass of water and took a deep breathe.

"Umm.... I'm ready to talk", he said without looking at me. "Okay...let's go and sit in the living room", I was ready to go, but he blocked me. "No, let's just talk here", he really wanted this conversation in the kitchen...I fold my hands and nod at him.

"What happened that night, I was not in my right mindset. I was.....it was because of my past", he looks at me.

"Jason, the years spent with Charles were unbearable for me. Because the abuse was unbearable. That night....that night it triggered my past too Jason. Have you really thought about me how much I really wanted to forget what you did to me? I saw Charles in you......I tried my best to forget you Jason but you were always there in my mind. I know there's a other side of story too".

"Are you going to share it with me or you still don't trust me enough", I said in a calm tone. I needed to be patient with him. "It's not because I don't trust you , it's...just that I'm scared", I see guilt all over his face.

"Jason, you know that I will never judge you, ever", I sigh in defeat and look down.

"It started when I was 7 years old.....

Chapter - 22 - The Real Truth

J ason

Warning this chapter includes child abuse and sexual assault

She thinks I don't trust her. She's wrong. I'm just a fucking coward. She has the right to know about everything. She doesn't deserve any of these. I don't care what she thinks, but I need to tell her the truth.

"It started when I was 7 years old..... We are a big family. For my grandfather, family is everything. He just wanted everyone to lead a healthy and happy life. My f-fa.....", I took a deep breath. I closed my eyes......I feel a soft touch on my shoulder. I opened my eyes.....she was in front of me. She didn't said anything but I felt like she was saying that she is with me.

This was enough for me to proceed. "My f-father, 'Victor Knight', and my uncle both worked together for the company.We were the picture perfect family. We used to be so happy. I had a good relationship with my father. Everything was going well, b-but my father started to act weird. He rarely used to come home, or any of our family occasions. My mama was worried about him, because he didn't spend time with us, but she was always there for me and Arlo. Arlo was just 3 years old. We both used to play and have fun", I smile while remembering the memories.

But my smile drops down as I further continue, "One day my mother decided to meet Victor in his office. S-she......she caught him cheating on her......with his secretary. She w-was broken, completely shattered. I never saw my mother so broken. She forgot her own dreams for him and he cheated on her. I remember our whole family was devastated because of him. Everyone got to know about his affair through media", I look at her and she was already looking at me with a sad face.

"He started blaming everything on my mother. But my grandfather trusted my mother more than him. After many arguments they finally came up with the divorce. My mother wanted the custody of mine and Arlo. But Victor didn't back down. He said he wanted to take custody of mine. He said he will not sign the divorce papers if he didn't had anyone's of our custody".My hands started to shake when I remember everything. Kira placed her hand on top of mine.

She gives me a small nod, so I can continue, "My mother eventually got the custody of Arlo because he was small. Mine was a tough one. My case took more time than Arlo's case. But Victor knew that my mother will win the custody of mine too, because he cheated on her. One day he came to me and said that he missed me. We both had a perfect father and son bonding. My mother didn't wanted this to happen. At that time period I used to live with him. My grandfather fired him from his own company. I was just a kid I didn't understand anything, but I really thought that Victor would take a good care of me".An unwanted chuckle escapes from my lips, realizing that I was so stupid back then.

"My family got disturbed because of him. The other night he just took me to another city and my family had no idea about it. He wanted to escape from the mess that he created. Things were not easy for him. As he struggled to get a job. His so called secretary was also living with us. No doubt, she always treated me as a burden, but because of my father she kept quiet. Victor was an egoistic man, he didn't like to be worked under someone. Everything started to be messy".I take a moment to calm my emotions.

Her hand is on top of mine. She runs her thumb back and forth and soon it relaxes me. I hurt her so bad, but here she is.....always by my side, comforting me. "Victor couldn't keep up with the job nor any company wanted to hire him because of his reputation. His girlfriend got a job and he was jobless. They both started having fights and arguments with each other. One day she just packed her bags and left and said that she doesn't want to live with him because he had no money and said that she was fed up of me.

My legs started shaking. My whole body was shaking in pure fear as I continue to tell her further.

"I think you are tired. It's enough for today, you sh____"."No", I stop her. I know it's going to bring all memories back, but it's more important to tell her the truth.

"I'm fine. Do you have beer or wine? I think I really need some", I lean back and take the support of the kitchen counter. "Umm.....you go back to the living room, I will bring up, okay?", she said. "Okay", I said and leave the kitchen. I take a seat on sofa and try to calm myself down.

He was so caught up with his mistakes that he didn't even bother to enroll me in a school.

She brought a bottle of wine and takes a seat beside me. I drink some, until I was ready and I started to speak again. "Victor was all alone. He used all the money in gambling. He started drinking continuously whether it was day or night. From there, he started treating me like trash. He started to take out his anger on me by scolding me. But days went by, when I was not allowed to go out of the house".I still remember everything as if it was happened yesterday.

"He started to put restrictions on me. He always used to say that because of my mother and me, his life was destroyed. He even used to blame me that because of me, his girlfriend left him alone. He started beating me. I was just 7 years old, he didn't......he didn't e-even think o-once about me. He used to hit me like I was an object to him. He played loud music so that nobody can hear my cries".I beg him to let me go, but he didn't care about anything. Kira was comforting me but I don't look at her.

"Everyday.....everyday w-was the s-same routine. The house......it became l-like a p-prison to me. He forcced me to do all the house works like cleaning, and even cooking. I-If the food was burnt....or he didn't liked it, he used to beat me. Day by day his actions were getting worse. He.......He started hitting with wooden bat, belts, steel rods. Sometimes he also used knife until I bleed.....a-and then just leave me".Those scenes play in my mind again, and it brought all my fears back. I try to take deep breaths and try to stop my tears.

"He got involved with drug dealers and criminals. The place were I live was no a home for me. It was always crowed with people and have late night parties. I was no longer a son to him. Days went by, I accepted the beating he gave me. I thought it was my fate. It was more worse if I try to escape from him. Some days, I used to strave, but he didn't care".I run my hand through my hair, my throat is dry and my stomach churns thinking about my past.

"Come here", I hear her voice and a look up at her. She extends her hand to me and give me a sad smile. I remove my shoes and lay my head on her lap and she runs her fingers through my hair, that relaxes me instantly.

"This went for 3 years..... and I was 10 year old. He was having late night party in the house. As usual I was serving them drinks and cleaning the stuff. A man was watching me continuously and he came up to me and grabbed my arm, I struggled to get out from his grip. Victor stopped him, they were rambling about something. The man said that he will give him money. My father looked at me and nodded back to him".I never thought my situation would get any more worse than that.

"Victor, took me to a room. I was shocked because I was not allowed to sleep in bed. I used to sleep on floor. The man before I saw, came to the room and handed money to Victor. Then, I knew what was going to happen with me. I begged Victor..... I even said that I could take his beatings, but he just kicked me in my stomach and left the room. Then.......He.....I-I was...r-raped by the man".I couldn't stop myself anymore. I felt tears in my eyes.

I clean them and continue, "I-I didn't know, why this was happening with me. He became greedy day by day. He wanted money, he used to invite his friends and sell me to his buddies. Everyday was a torture for me. I didn't even knew, when was the last time I saw the sun. It was painful......so much painful. I used to shout, but they didn't stop. Nobody heard my cries or came to help me. E-even......sometimes, there would be m-more than t-two men, they were all merciless. They didn't stop when I used to bleed and pass out".

I felt drops of tears on my cheek. I look up at her, tears were running down from her eyes. "Jason I am sorry, but I-I can't____".I look at her and wipe her tears from her face.

"It's okay, you don't have to be sorry", I interlock my hand with hers."No Jason, I am sorry. You suffered so much and I pressurized you", she said. "No baby, you were right in your place and I should have shared it with you a long time ago", I kiss her hand.

"Jason, how did you escaped from him?", she asked. "Well, I was 13 year old by then. He used to be highly intoxiated. I wanted to see the world, I wanted to go outside in the sun. I wanted to fight for me at least one time, I had nothing to lose. One day he forgot to lock my room. I thought this was my chance to escape. I slowly made out of the room and I saw he was watching television. I just wanted to escape, but he saw me and grabbed me by my hair. I took a lamp beside the table and smashed on his head. He started bleeding. I immediately ran from the house. It was late night I ran as fast as I can. I didn't even turn behind once, I just wanted to be free. But I didn't have much energy and I was tired and the next moment I knew I passed out. I don't remember anything, but the next day I found myself in the hospital".I saw the sun was coming through the window and shinning bright on my face. I never thought I would see it again.

I took a short pause and continued, "As I opened my eyes I saw Doctors and Cops around me. I was terrified by their presence and I hide myself in the blanket. But they were calm and patient with me. They found me in the middle of road, and saw all the marks on my body. They said that they will help me. So I told them everything......they all were shocked. Few cops went to check the place......but of course he was not there. But they said that they saw his blood on the floor. Then they contacted my family. They started to find Victor. By evening my family arrived and I saw my mother after so many years. As the moment she saw me she started crying and my grandpa too. She was talking to me but I didn't respond, I was quite. I thought it was a dream. I didn't spoke to anyone and they respected that. My family knew what happened to me....everyone was shocked. My mother blamed herself for what happenmed with me.

Kira kissed my hand and runs her fingers through my hair."After what happened with me I became distant to everyone. I didn't like if someone used to be closed to me. Every night I had nightmares of him torturing me".I run my thumb at back of her hand. "Why where you afraid to tell me?", she asked. Because I was over thinking. I got up from her and sit close beside her. "I.......I thought... after knowing what happened to me, you would leave me", I didn't look at her and she palced her hand on my face and made me look at her.

"Why?", her eyes never left mine. Because I was stupid and idiot.

"M-My w-whole body is tainted. I'm tainted. I hate my body, I always cover it up. After knowing about my past and about my nightmares, no doubt everyone will think I'm a coward. Even I can say that I'm not brave. Why anyone would stay with some coward, who cries everynight. Every women thinks and dreams of a man who can protect her and keep her safe. But.....but I think I failed in that too", I didn't look at her nor did she said anything.

"I....I don't want you to pity me, nor I want you to forgive me. I....I just want a second chance. That night I planned dinner for us. I was going to confess my feelings to you...but I saw Victor. I don't know how....the face, the man that haunted me, was right in front of me. I don't know if he recognised me or not, but I was scared. I was not in my right mindset. I didn't knew what was happening with me. I thought he was you and I......", I took a moment. I don't know how to say this to her. I really can't explain the situation to her, so I just close my eyes. I don't know what she is going to say, but at the end she is always going to be the only woman I love.

"Jason, you are the one who I want. You protect me, take care of me and you love me. That's what's important for me".After everything she still choose me and love me. What did I ever do, that I got her.Kira Regina White. My Kira....My baby.

She cupped my face in her hands, "You were a kid Jason and yet you fought till the end. You are so brave____"."But Kira_____"No Jason. I want every single part of you, the good and the bad. I want everything of yours to be mine. I want you......

Hey guys!! I know it's been a long time since I updated. I'm sorry I had some important stuff that needed to be taken care of. But anyways thank you so much for being patient with me. Please keep supporting because it means a lot to me.

Chapter - 23 - Family Gatherings

K IRA

I was thinking so wrong about him. I never thought he would have suffered so much. This is the reason, he was hiding his past from me. He thought I will judge him or leave him. He thinks he will not able to protect me. Past few days, I was thinking only about myself, but how much had he suffered these days?

I was so selfish. Bringing up the past memories, he went through the pain again because of me."It doesn't change anything between us. Now your pain is mine. We will go through this together". I interwine our hands.

"Do you forgive me?", he asked. "I forgive you, Jason. From now on, we will share everything and no more secrets", he nods at me. "I think we should go slow. We can also start over and maybe you can fall in love with me again", he said.

"I am already in love with you Laszlo", I smile at him. "I love you too Kira, so much", he wraps his arms around me and give me a warm hug. God, I missed him so much. I nuzzle my face in his chest more. We stayed in each others arms for sometime, no one saying anything to each other.

After sometime we break apart, "I think I should leave now, It's late", he gets up from the sofa. I think I should tell him to stay. Should I? I don't know?

"Your friends still didn't came?",he doesn't look at me. "No April message me that they are going to be late"."Ohh...I...They must be hating me, for...for what I did to you", he runs his hand through his hair. "No, they don't know what exactly happened between us because I didn't tell anybody", I said and he gave me a confused look.

"Why?", he held his head down."Because it happened between us, and I didn't wanted any person to know about it. I didn't wanted to tell your mistake to the world, I just wanted you to be honest with me", I held his hand in mine.

"I really don't deserve you. You're way to good for me. But I can't let you go now", he smiles down at me."Good night Kira", he kisses my forehead and leaves. I can still smell his scent. I really should've said him to stay. But I think we both should take it slow.

____

Things have been very much better this passed few days. Both me and Laszlo are having a good understanding between us. We have been going out for dates and spending evenings with each other and even hanging out with our friends.

I realized that Laszlo deserves everything in this world. He deserves to be cared, happy and loved. And I will make sure that I will give him everything he needs.

"Why are you staring at me", Jason smirks at me.Well,we are in the park right now and we are sitting under tree where is he reading a book for me, while I'm in his arms and resting my head on his chest. He wraps one hand around me and holding a book in another hand and rest his back on the huge tree.

"So what, I can't look at my boyfriend now?", I kiss his neck and smile at him. "Of course baby. I'm yours. You can look at me unless you want to do some other things to me", he winks at me and I smack his chest and he laughs. We didn't have sex but he gives me really good pleasures.

"I wanted to talk to you about something?", I said to him. I have been willing to tell him but I couldn't. I think this is a good time. "Me too. You go first", he said.

I sit up I am really nervous right now. I've been thinking about this fre-quently and...I-I____"Are you breaking up with me?", he cuts me of in middle."No, what----why would I break up with you? Jesus, you didn't even let me complete"."Fuck. Thank god, I thought you were going to", he rest his head on my shoulder. He is really clingy, not that I complain.

"Now you are not going to say anything stupid till I complete", I shake my head and take a deep breath."I am thinking about this from few days Laszlo, y-you are still having nightmares at night. It really pains me to see you in pain and crying in my arms. I know that I comfort you and I want to comfort you. But I also want to take your pain away. You need to get healed", he doesn't say anything he just stares at me.

"Where this is all going baby, I don't understand", he give me a sad smile.I cup his cheek, "Laszlo, I have a friend and she's a great therapist. She has dealt with many cases including abuse and sexual assault and outcomes have been really good. I want you to go to the therapy. It's not only about me Laszlo, but the other people in your life. Because if you never heal from what hurt you, you'll bleed on people who didn't cut you", I see tears in corner of his eyes.

"I-I will go to the therapy for you", he gives me a smile. "No Laszlo, it's not for me. You will do it for yourself, my love. Healing doesn't have to look magical. Real healing is hard, exhausting and draining. Let yourself go through it. Be there for yourself without judgement". I kiss his forehead and close my eyes and rest my forehead against his.

"You are really on a mission to make me cry, don't you?", he laughs. "I guess I am", I chuckle. "I will go and do it for myself. How about I start up from tomorrow", I didn't thought this would go this easy. But here he is, my man, my love.

"Okay, I will contact my friend and set up therapy sessions for you", I peck his lips. I almost forgot, he said he wanted to say something too. "You said you wanted to say something too, right?"."Ahh, yes of course. Actually it's kind of important too".

"Go ahead", I said. "My family knows that I've a girlfriend now as I'm spending time with you everyday. My mother was very upset aand angry with me after she knew what happened between us. And now we are together again....my family has invited you for dinner tomorrow. Everyone is excited to meet you especially my Mama. She's dying to meet you", I don't know what to say.

It's not that I don't want to meet them but the dinner is tomorrow and he us telling me now!!!I punch his arm hard and he flinched in pain.

"Ouch!!What was that for? ", he asked. "You are telling me now. I don't have anything to wear for tomorrow. Oh my god...I need to go for shopping with April. There are so many things I need to take care of...and I have a night shift tomorrow, how I_______", he cuts me in middle again.

"Relax baby, you are rambling. Don't worry about anything I will take care of it. You literally have so many clothes in your closet. If not I will buy it for you", he said in duhh tone.

"Excuse me mister? What does that mean? Let me remind you your family is just like the royal family. Everyone of your family are literally in all fucking magazines. Of course I want to make a good impression on your them and you will not buy anything for me", I look at his face and I can clearly see that he is holding his laugh.

And now he is laughing at me. Great. "You should look at your face. Shit, I'm sorry but I can't hold it anymore", I can't believe this man. What's so funny about this?

"Look, I-I know your nervous. But don't worry about this so much. The dinner is tomorrow babe. You have plenty of time, so just relax and enjoy the evening with me", he wraps his arm around me. "You are so lucky, that I love you", I said and rest my head again on his chest. "Don't I know that", he chuckles.

———————————

"Does it look good? Is it too much?", I'm so nervous right now. I don't know what's gonna happen but I know that for Jason, his family is important to him and I don't want to give a bad impression of them. "You are looking so beautiful. I love this dress. They are gonna love you, Don't worry about that", he shrugs. Yeah, easy for him to say that. I hope everything goes well.

We reach his home. This is so fucking big and huge than his own bunglow. He takes my hand in his, "Are you ready? Don't worry, just be yourself. I'm sure they are gonna love you ", he smiles.

"Okay", he then pulls me close and plant his lips on mine. He kisses me slow and soft. "I think that's enough. You both can go inside now", we get interrupted by none other than Liam.

"Way to ruin a romantic moment asshole", Jason throws him a sarcastic smile. "Welcome bitch", he glares back at Jason. And they both laugh. I'm really nervous right now, and these men are cracking jokes. Idiots.

"Seriously, why did you asked me to join dinner with your family",Liam asked Jason."I have a new job for you and this is your family too", Jason gives him a hug. "Let's go before you kiss me too",Liam runs inside the house."Asshole", Jason shouts back at him.

He holds my hand again and kisses my forehead and we enter his house. Wow they really live like a royal family. The interior was so amazing with really expensive furnitures and designing. I am way out of the standards. There where so many maids, workers and bodyguard inside the house.

"Finally look at both of you. You both looks so lovely together", Mrs Knight is the first one to greet us.She hugged Jason and then surprisingly she pulls me for hug too. She look so pretty at this age to.

"You are looking more beautiful than a first meet you. How are you, my dear?",bshe holds my both hands in her."I am good. Thank you for inviting me to dinner Mrs Knight".

"Call me Julia ,dear. We all wanted to meet you. Come with me, I will introduce you to the rest of our family", she pulls me with her leaving Jason behind. He is having a very big family. I greet everyone of them. They were so nice to me and his grandfather 'Henry Knight' he was so fun to be around.

It went so much better than I expected it to be. I met his uncle, aunt and their kids. They all were really so good with me. We had dinner together.

I was so happy. I felt like I was a part of their family from long time ago. I really had a good time.

"Aunt Janella, when is Aliana arriving?", Jason questioned his aunt. "She messaged me. She should be here now", his aunt replied and Jason just nodded. "Who is Aliana by the way?", I asked Jason. "Aliana is Aunt Janella's daughter as in my cousin sister, she went for one week trip with her friends", he said.

We all were in the living room chatting with each other. A beautiful young girl entered the living room with her luggage. I think she must be Aliana. Everyone greeted her and then she came to us.

"How was your trip?",Jason asked her."It was really amazing. Now introduce me to your girlfriend", she looks at me."Aliana meet Kira my girlfriend. Kira, she is my sister Aliana", she instantly pull me for hug. Yep everyone of their family really likes to hug.

"It's nice to meet you. You are very pretty",she compliments me. "Thanks ,you are beautiful too",I said."There's something I want to tell you", Jason said to Aliana. He calls Liam who was busy talking with other bodyguards.

Liam joined us. And I look between Liam and Aliana , I felt like there was something between them that I am not sure of. "Liam from now on you are going to protect Aliana. You are her new bodyguard", Jason said. "What the fuck? Why him? I-I don't need anyone to protect me", Aliana fought back.

"No, Jason it's not fair. I mean she is s nightmare , and she is just a kid"."I am not a kid, I'm gonna be 20 this year"."It's still counts 19, genius", they both started arguing with each other. I was holding my laugh. They both looked so cute while arguing with each other.

"Enough!!No more arguing. It's final. It's better you both get along with it", Jason declares himself. Leaving no room for them to say. Jason leaves to talk with his mother. I look between both Aliana and Liam. They both are staring at each other like they will kill each other any time. Fuck, why I am stuck here.

I clear my throat to break the silence. "Aliana, it would be great if we can meet sometime", I said and she smiled at me and gave me a hug. "Of course, I'd love it", and then she looks at Liam, "I'm gonna talk to grandpa about this", she says and leaves.

Liam is still staring at her. I playfully look at Liam. "You like her, don't you?", I said. "Are you out of your mind. She bothers me so much. And she's 19", he scoffs and shakes his head. "Okay, suit yourself. We will see about that", I said and he gives me a confused look and I laugh.

I search for Jason in his huge mansion. I don't understand where did he go. "He went searching for you too", I turned back. Jason's mother was smiling at me. "Come dear, I will give you a tour of the house", she grabs my hand and takes me with her.

She literally showed me every corner of their huge mansion. It's kinda funny how they call this as their house. It's a freaking huge mansion.

We are currently walking in the hallway. We talked about so many things. "I know what happened between both of you", she took a pause, "I'm sorry for what he did to you. I was really mad at him. But he realised his mistake and he was guilty. I think he told about his past to you. I'm really sorry Kira. You didn't deserve that", she said. She is really kind just like how Jason tells me about her.

"You don't need to. Everything is better now. When he told me about his side of story, I got to know how hard, it must have been for him. I forgive him Julia. Thanks for your concern though", I smile at her and she does the same too.

"He said to me that now he's going for therapy sessions. Today was his first day. He is really happy. He just talks about you, how you are helping him. I think I failed to do that job, but seeing that you're with him and talking care of him is more than enough for me. Thank you Kira", I can see tears in her eyes.

"I'm sorry if it makes you uncomfortable...but do you really think he saw his father that night", I asked. "I don't know Kira. He just disappeared when cops went to check the house. They searched him for months. He was no where to be found", she takes a deep breathe.

"But I know Jason would never lie. But if he is really back...I'm with him and his whole family and even you now", she gives me a small smile.

"Can you promise me that you will be with him for rest of his life. He needs you so much. I'm finally seeing my son so happy and interacting with everyone. I know he can be annoying sometimes", we both laugh, "You are like a light to his life Kira", I wipe her tears.

"You are really making me cry. I promise Julia, I will always be with him. I need him in my life too. I love him".

"There you are. I was searching for________Am I Interrupting something ", he comes beside me. "No, I was just giving Kira a tour to our house", Julia said. "Mama, it's late. I think we should leave", he said. Julia nods and again she gives us a tight hug. We said goodbye to everyone.

We are waiting for the driver to bring the car. Jason stares me with lust filled in his eyes. "What are you looking at?", I asked. "I'm just thinking what I should so with you when we reach home", he smirks. I think I'm already wet down there. You can't blame me. It's been long time since we had sex.

He comes closer to me and wispers down my ears."First, I'm going to tear this dress of your body and take my time to worship your body. I will make your body shake with pleasure as I pound intk you", he kissed under my ear.

"I can't wait to get home",he said looking at me.

A shiver runs down my spine just thinking about it.

Chapter - 24 - Mine

☐ ☐This chapter contains mature content.

JASON

Everything is getting so better now. I finally introduced Kira to my family. They all were so happy for me. She literally was nervous to meet them, but my family is always welcoming and friendly. I knew they would love her.

She's trying to make me a better person for myself. The way she cares for me.....no one in my life has ever did that. I'm so fucking lucky that she loves me. I'm so grateful that she is in my life.

I still remember the moment when she said she loves me. I couldn't believe when I heard that.....she doesn't know what kind of effect she has on me. There are so many precious moments, that happened between us in last few days. There was this one.....

After she finished her working hours in the hospital, we decided to go for a walk. It was pretty late at night. We talked about so many things. She used to talk about how her day went or discuss about random things. I only used to hear her voice.

The way she interlock our hands and watches the stars above us. The way she laughs or giggles in between our conversation, always made my heart beat faster for her. When we reached home, she was tired. After some time we both cuddled in the bed. I wrapped my arms around her as she was on top of me.

"It's so hot today, how are you wearing a shirt? Infact, you always wear a shirt around me", she pout her lips. I kissed her lips and sigh. Now Kira knows about my past and last few days, I didn't cover up my scars....So I just wear a shirt when she is around, so that she doesn't get uncomfortable.

"I-I.....I don't want y-you to get uncomfortable when you s-see my scars", I tighten my arms around her and hide my face in her hair. She moves out my arms and I close my eyes. But she gets on top of me, I can feel her cupping my cheeks in her hands and rubs her thumb back and forth.

"Laszlo, look at me", I open my eyes and she pecks my lips. "I love you Laszlo, that means I love every part of you. You don't need to hide your scars from anyone. And you don't need to hide it from me", she kissed all over my face which made me smile.

"I'm sorry", she whispers. Why is she saying sorry? She didn't do anything. "I'm sorry because I should've talked this with you a long time ago. But baby, don't hide your scars from me or anyone. As I always say...be yourself".

"B-But....I...They are ugly. My body is ugly. They always remained me of how coward and weak I am"."No Laszlo, never be ashamed of a scar. It simply means you were stronger than whatever tried to hurt you", she leans her forehead against mine and cupped my face in her hands.

"You really make me feel so better with your words. Thank you so much baby", I started kissing her neck. But she gets up and also pulls me with her. She plays with my shirt buttons and she looks up at me, "Can I?", she asked for my permission.

I nod at her and she started unbuttoning my shirt. I instantly close my eyes, I was afraid to see her reaction. She slowly removed my shirt off my body. I can feel her hands on my chest. She touched every scar on my body. It felt weird because no body has ever saw or touched my scars before.

She saw that it made me feel uneasy. She started placing small kisses on each and every scars of mine. I opened my eyes and she was already looking at me. I saw her.....her eyes were filled with love. She kissed my forehead, "I love you so much Jason. Please don't forget that I'm always here for you. If you are ever worried about something, promise me that you'll talk to me", she sighs.

She rests her head on my chest. She is my soulmate. What did I ever do to have her in my life? But she's only mine. My woman, my love, my Kira.

It is one of my precious memories with her.

____

She's looking so fucking hot in that dress. All night, I was thinking about the ways to fuck her tonight. I've literally had blue balls so many times.... and I'm tired of the cold showers. I know she wants me as much as I want her. I've already made up my mind that I'm gonna fuck her so hard that she will not able to walk for days.

We are waiting for my car to arrive, as soon as the driver drops us at my house, I'm gonna throw her over my shoulder...and I did. "Laszlo stop!! Drop me off. I swear if I fall---", "That mouth of yours is gonna get you into trouble and just wait until we reach the room", she gasps as I spank her ass.

I don't care about anything, I just rushed towards my bedroom. She didn't said anything because she knew what I am going to do with her.

As I reached my bedroom, I drop her on the bed and I started removing my suit, tie and started unbuttoning my shirt as she was watching me with lust filled in her eyes. "Are you enjoying the show baby?", I ask her. She bites her lips and nods at me. "Good, but it's just gonna be better", I said while removing my pants. I was just left with my boxers.

I don't want to waste anymore minute now. I caged her between my arms and I tore her new dress, her eyes went wide in shock, "Laszlo, I just bought it yesterday", she looks down at her torn dress, "and please don't say that you will buy me 10 more of this dress because you are a billi-------", I didn't let her complete and smashed my lips on her. I kissed her hard and bite her lips causing her to moan my name. My tongue collides with hers......she tastes so fucking sweet.

"I had to baby, I want you so bad", my fingers running her soft skin. I started placing kisses on her neck. I kiss my way down to her breasts and unhooking her black lacy bra. My hands cup her breast and I rub my thumb around her nipples. They are so hard right now.

I take one of her nipple in my mouth and suck it hard, she grabs my hair tight in her hands. I gave both of her breasts the same attention. She moans out loudly.

"Look at you baby, already so wet for me", I slide her underwear off her body. "You are so beautiful Kira", I moved my hands from her stomach to down her pussy. I pushed my finger on her clit and slowly rubbed circles on it.

"Keep going", my baby moans out loudly. I insert my two fingers inside her, she throws her head back in pleasure. I started going faster and she was on the edge of her pleasure, and that's when I removed my fingers. She really thought I will go easy on her?.

"Why did you do that?", I smirked at her. "Now you know, how I felt the whole dinner when you kept rubbing your body against mine.""Laszlo, I didn't-------", "I don't care baby, I'm going to keep you up all night", I whisper, placing a soft kiss on her lips.

"Now, open your legs", she follows my order. I latch my mouth straight onto her pussy. I suck her hard and she grabs my hair tightly. I bite her clitoris and her angelic moan escapes from her lips."Don't stop Laszlo", that's when the evil thought comes upto my mind. I know she is on the edge and I stop again.

She is really pissed off now. "Laszlo, don't do this to me", she covers her face with her hands. "You are my good girl, aren't you?", she instantly nods her head. I chuckle at her eagerness.

"You are going to be a good girl and take my dick, right?", I ask her. "Yes Laszlo", she moans out, as I run my fingers around her clit. "Tell me baby, what do you want?", she rolls her hips against my fingers. "I-I.....I want you Laszlo, please....".

This was it. I remove my boxers and I'm already hard for her. I bring my hard dick towards her were pussy and rub it against her clit. "Please Laszlo, stop teasing me", I chuckle and she gasp when I slam into her.

She's so fucking tight. I don't even let her adjust to my size as I pound into her relentlessly. Sweet moans comes out of her mouth and throws her head back in pleasure. Tears stream down her beautiful face as I relentlessly thrust in and out of her.

"More Laszlo", she tightens her legs around my waist. "Fuck Kira, you feel so good baby, clench your pussy around me", I grunt and put her leg over my shoulder and fuck her deep in this position.

"Y-Yes Laszlo, I'm going to cum", I bite her nipples and suck it hard as they were swollen red. "You will wait for me, right baby?", she bites my neck as she is on the edge of her pleasure. I couldn't hold it anymore. I kiss her neck and make my way up to her lips. "Cum with me baby", with that I swallow all her moans. I cum inside her and she cums with me.

I can hear her breathing, "Don't fall asleep now, I'm going to keep you all night", I said and kissed her.

____

I think it's more than 4 hours now. I never really knew that I had this much stamina. But watching my baby cuming around my dick and hearing her sweet moans, is what keeping me on. I thrust one last time and release my cum inside her again. She is already tired, so I went to bathroom and bring a wet towel and clean her up.

I lay down beside her and adjust her on top of me, as she lays her head on my chest. "Do you need anything baby?", I ask her but she shakes her head. She draws small patterns on my chest with her fingers.

"You really didn't had a girlfriend?", she questions me. "I already told you baby, I was never in a relationship", I hold her tight in my arms. "That means I don't have to deal with anyone?", she looks up at me. "What do you mean?"."You know like how they show in movies, a rich billionaire has a ex-girlfriend and then she sabotages his current relationship", she smirks.

I chuckle, "As I said to you, I only used to work and never really had a reason to date someone. And I only used to have meaningless hookups. None of them satisfied me like you do", I replied her while looking at the ceiling.

"I didn't asked you about that", she smacks my chest but after a pause she said, "That means I have no competition?", I laugh and cup her cheeks.

"There is no competition for you Kira. Because no one, I repeat no one in this world would make me feel, as you do. I'm yours baby. You don't need to worry about anyone else. I fell in love with you because you loved me when I couldn't love myself. I know being with me is not easy, but I want you to understand no one has me, or has ever had me, except you".

I look in her eyes. I kiss her forehead. She has a huge smile on her face and rest her head on my chest again. So fucking cute.

I run my hands through her hair, "Infact I'm the one who is afraid. I've never been so scared of losing something in my life, then again, nothing in my life has ever meant as much to me as you do", I take a pause, "I'm afraid someone is going to make you happier than I do. I'm sorry I ever dragged you into my twisted, messed up world. Please don't stop loving me, please don't ever leave me."

She didn't said anything. I look down, she's already asleep. I smile and hold her as close as possible and kiss her forehead.

"I almost lost you once. God, you don't have any idea how that felt, not being close to you or hold you in my arms. I fear because, something so great won't happen twice. And you are the greatest thing that ever happened in my life. There is only one thing I want you to do------never give up on me."

I'm never letting her go. I love her so much.

Chapter - 25 - Ball Night

K IRA

I got so tired yesterday. I remember talking with Jason, but the next moment I just slept. You can't blame me. Seriously, that man really has an incredible stamina, no wonder he works 24/7. I slowly open my eyes, and I was all alone in the room.

Jason was not there beside me and I was in his shirt. Jason must have dressed me. I was ready to move out of bed but flinched in pain. Fuck, I'm really sore down there. It's like my legs have lost the energy to walk. Anyways, I try to get down, but the door opens and there comes the most handsome man I ever saw.

I can say that he just showered because of his wet hair. They are slightly on his forehead. He wore a simple grey t-shirt and sweat pants. He brought breakfast for me. He has a huge smile on his face. He kept the breakfast beside me and sat down next to me.

"Good morning, how are you feeling?", he tucks my hair behind my ear. "Good morning. I'm a little sore. I think I can't walk properly. What time is it?".

"Baby, it's eleven", he rolls his eyes. "Shit!!! I'm so late. I need to go now------", I was ready to get out of bed despite of the pain, but Jason grabs my shoulder, "Relax Kira, don't worry about your work", easy for him to say this. I hold his hands. "Laszlo, if I don't get up now, Dr. Ron will eat up my job", I say in a serious tone.

"I knew you would be worried about it, so I talked with him. He doesn't have any problem", he shruggs his shoulder. How the fuck does he handled this? It's not the first time he said this. Dr. Ron is known for his mean and strict behavior. He doesn't goes easy on anyone. And nowadays his behavior towards me is completely different. Before he was really rude and strict and now he talks politely with me and he just smiles. And that is so fucking weird.

I know that Jason is the reason behind this. "What did you told him Laszlo?", I asked him. He opens and close his mouth, thinking about what he should answer. "Laszlo?", I glared at him. "Nothing, just casual talk. Why don't you eat-----", "Jason!!!", I shout out his name. Now he knows that I'm serious about it.

"Okay okay...I....I may.....I may have threatened him", he whispers but I hear it. I am shocked and he just avoids my gaze. I can't believe this man."Are you out of your mind!!!Do you have any idea what you did?", he is still not looking at me.

I grab him by his shirt, "You can't do that Jason I-----", he cuts me off in middle. "Laszlo baby, call me Laszlo", he grins at me. He is clearly distracting me. "You are turning me on babe", he leans forward, his lips are brushing mine. I was nearly falling in his trap, but then it suddenly hits me and I push him back.

"Don't you dare try to seduce me", he winks at me. "I'm serious Laszlo. You can't keep doing that I can handle him, you don't need to do any of this. Not all days should go good and happy. Sometimes it's okay to have a bad day. Dr. Ron, he is my boss and he has every right to shout on me if I do anything wrong. It's part of my job. Promise me, you won't do this again", I hold his hands in mine.

"I know that he is your boss, but that doesn't mean that he has the right to say anything rubbish about you. And that guy is the biggest scumbag I ever met. You don't know Kira, but that man doesn't eat your job but he eats all the money and do nothing. I won't promise you that, because if anyone says anything about my woman, I will make sure he or she will regret it", there's no point to fight on this with him.

"You'll be the end of me", I kiss his hand and his cute smile appears on his face. "Now pick me up, I need to freshen up", I open my arms for him. He chuckles and picks me up. I got freshen up and sat for breakfast. He said that he already ate before I woke up.

As I was finished eating the food, he said, "Will you attend a ball party with me?", he asked. "Umm..what kind of ball?", he is massaging my leg. It really fees good. "Well, it is a party held by my business partner. And he has invited every rich businessman and famous peoples. My family is going to be there too. Mama said that she wants you there and....me too."

Of course, I've never been to a party with rich people. I don't know anyone. I barely knew Jason before we met. What I am going to do between those rich people. "I will think about it", his smile falls down but he nods hospital head. "Yeah, of course. Do you want some more pancakes?", he changed the topic. I'm glad he did.

Me and April went to restaurant. I missed her. After finishing with our food, we went to our apartment. We sat down in our living room and I told her everything what Jason said.

"Bitch, that's a great news!!! What are you worried about?", she is sitting in front of me. "We are middle class families, April. That party is for rich peoples and it's not going to be easy for me", I sigh.

"Did Jason talked about this with you?", she asked. " No.""Did he told you to change yourself?"."What....no.""Did he ever judged you about your work or your livingstyle? "."Of course not!!!", Jason never judged me for any of these. He just loves me the way I am.

"Then what's the problem babe?", she throws a pillow at me. "People, Media and Charles, April.""What about that stupid asshole.""Media's gonna be there. And eventually he gonna know about me. You know how he followed us everywhere and I don't want him to know."April ways her hand to stop me but I don't.

"I'm a simple girl...and he is a huge businessman. Our worlds are totally different. His one month salary is equal to our more than one year's salary. And people are gonna label me as a golddigger who is after him. They're gonna think I'm sleeping with him for his money and fame. It's just not that easy", I sigh and look at April. She is already standing and shocked. .

"Kira, I think you should turn back. "Oh god no. Please don't be him. As I turn I see Jason with my favorite flowers in his hand. I instantly regretted what I said. I should've locked the door.

I don't know how much he has heard but he is hurt. I saw him clenching his fists. I slowly approach towards him. "Jason I------", "Glad to hear what to think about us", he drops the flowers on the table. He leaves and shuts the door harshly.

"Kira, fuck the people and fuck your ex-boyfriend. Babe, he is fighting for you since he met you. He is doing everything, just to keep you happy. That guy is madly in love with you. He loves you so much and you're a idiot to not to see that", she comes in front of me and grabs my shoulder.

"He doesn't care about the media or the so called people. He just cares about you and you should do the same Kira. Enough using your mind and follow your heart."

I just process everything April said. She's right. Jason always cares about me. He doesn't care what people say because he loves me. "Kira I think you should go now!! I think he's waiting for you", she says while peeking out of the window. I grab everything and tightly hug April and thanked her.

I run as fast as I can and I see him near his car. His back is resting against the car. I can clearly see that he's angry with me. As I slowly approach to him, he grabs my shoulder and caged me. My back is resting against the car and he has caged me in his arms.

"Jason, I----", "No, you listen to me. I know that you are scared of your stupid ex-boyfriend, because I too also know how it feels like", he takes a step back and runs his hand through his hair.

"Kira there are always gonna be those people who will judge us and talk bad things about us. They are not just two or three of them but they will be thousands of them. That doesn't mean we are not good for each other, that doesn't mean we will stop being happy. For me only thing matters is that we both love each other. It hurts me that you care about others but not me."

"I know that, I'm sorry. I really want to go to the ball with you, but I'm scared that what if I embarrass you? I don't want to cause any problems to you because of me", tears runs down my cheek. He comes near me and wipe my tears away.

"I'm here with you. You will never cause any problem to me. Even that guy, whatever that fuckers name is, I will be here and I'm gonna protect you", he hugs me and I bury my face in his chest.

"Please don't cry Kira. It's okay", he pats my back. "For god's sake, please don't tell me that, the ball is tomorrow", he laughs. "No, it's next week. We have plenty of time", we both laugh. "My silly woman", he hugs me tighter.

____

April and Jason are right. As long as I have Jason with me I don't need to be worried about anything. And not to forget I apologized to Dr. Ron. I was not going to but when Jason told me that he pierced a pen in his thigh, the next moment I apologized. But Dr. Ron was so afraid of Jason, that he said it was all his fault. God I sometimes really can't understand these men.

The ball is today. We are getting ready. Julia called me and told me to attend the ball. It really feels good that she cares about me. Jason bought me a dress despite saying no to him. The dress is expensive, because it has rich fabric. It is a black split slip dress. It is really beautiful. He is waiting for me downstairs. I went down, he finally looked at me. "You look so gorgeous in this dress. We should leave or I will throw you over my shoulder again", he winked at me.

We are still in the car. I'm nervous right now. I watch through glass, people clicking photos. I've never faced that many cameras before. "It's okay. I usually don't talk to them. You don't need to say anything too. Shall we?", Jason kissed my hand and I nod at him.

When we got out, everyone started whispering. They thought Jason is going to be here alone. As nobody saw him before with any woman.

They started clicking photos and here we go. "Mr. Knight, is she your date?"."What's the name of your lovely date?"."Are you guys dating?".They started to ask many questions and there were so many camera flashes.

Jason was whispering sweet things in my ear. It really relaxed me in a way. We enter the building, "Are you okay?", he asked. I smile and nod at him. He leans down and kissed my lips."Eww, stop sucking each other faces now!!!", again it's none other than the famous 'Liam'. Jason breaks our kiss, rest his forehead against mine and sighs.

"Why this fucker always ruins our special moment", Jason punches his arm. "It's not my fault. You guys are always kissing each other when I'm around", he shruggs. "One day, you are gonna know how it feels", Jason said.

"By the way, your business partners are calling you", Jason nods. "Why are you not with Alianna?", Jason asked and Liam is annoyed. "She is with....her boyfriend", Liam scoffed the last part. "What!!Did you do a background check on him?"."Jason!!!", I shout.

"It's necessary baby", he turns to Liam. "We will talk about this later. Now stay beside Kira, I will be back shortly after meeting with the fuckers", they both laugh. 'Men'. Jason kissed my forehead and said he will be back in a moment and leaves.

Both me snd Liam talked for some minutes. I look at Liam, but he is looking somewhere else. I follow his gaze, without any doubt, I know he is looking at Alianna. She was dancing with a guy and Liam had a scowl on his face.

"Is that her boyfriend?", he is still looking at them. "Yeah, her dumbass boyfriend", he shakes his head. "Oh my god!! You are so jealous of her boyfriend", I laugh at him, he looks so funny.

"No, why would I be jealous", god I sometimes hate Liam, when he denies his feelings. Alianna saw me, and approached us, but she didn't bring her boyfriend with her. "You look so hot, Kira", she hugs me. "Please, you look way more hot than me", we laugh. She looks looks at Liam but doesn't say anything.

"Was that your boyfriend? He looks cool", I say and she nods her head. "Yeah. I hope Jason will accept him", she said and Liam chuckles. "First of all, where did you meet him?", Liam asked but she doesn't respond.

"Do you really think you have any right to date any boys you want?", I snap my head towards Liam and shake my head to stop him but he doesn't. "Because at last everybody knows that it's your mom, who pushed you into this relationship with that idiot. So stop pretending that you are in love with him". Alianna eyes are covered in tears, he is really a dumbass. But he regretted saying it when he saw her tears.

She went close to him. I know I shouldn't say this, but fuck it literally felt like I was watching a drama scene. "Well, there's one good thing about it. At least that idiot I'm dating is isn't you", fuck this girl came back so hard. I love her.

"That's my sister. I'm proud of you", Arlo approaches us with champagne in his hand. He winks at me and I roll my eyes. Alianna shakes her head in annoyed way. "Idiot", she says to Arlo and she looks at Liam, "And fuck you", she storms away. "Come back here Alianna. Please, stop Dove", Liam follows her.

He got it so hard for her. I see Julius comes beside Arlo and greets me. I don't believe, why didn't he told me that he is also attending this ball with Arlo.I grab him by his ear, "Seriously, you could've told me that you are attending this party", I didn't leave his ear.

"Hey, stop pulling my boyfriend's ear", Arlo said, while Julius flinches in pain and I leave him. "Watch your tone, when you are talking with my girlfriend", Jason hugs me from behind and placed a kissed back of my ear, causing butterflies in my stomach.

"Good to see you back Arlo", Jason hugs him. Arlo and Julius spend a lot of time with each other. And recently they both went for a trip, that's why they didn't attend the family dinner. We talked and after some time Julia came and greeted us. I met some Jason's business partners. I met so many new people, and I still don't remember their names.

"Dance with me baby", Jason grabs my hand. "I really don't know how to dance", this is so embarrassing. "Just follow my lead", we both slowly swayed our bodies with the music. Jason buries his head in my neck and started placing small kisses. I was going to stop him but he said, "Before you say anything, let them watch I don't care", I blushed even harder.

After dancing, we were just talking with the people. "Jason, I need to go to washroom"."Okay, I will come with you"."No, it's okay". He nods and kissed my forehead.

I'm really tired, I don't know how people do this. I wash my hands. "Hello love", I know this voice. The voice I always wanted to forget. I look in the mirror and he is standing behind me.

"Aren't you gonna greet me? Where are you're manners darling? I knew you were a slut. Sleeping with the famous billionaire for his money. I think you should be punished."I wanted to shout but couldn't. My throat went dry. He slowly approaches me. "Don't come near me. Jason------", I shout out as loudly as I can, but he grabs me harshly and shuts my mouth with his hand.

Chapter - 26 - Her Ex-Boyfriend

JASON

I really wanted to spend all my time with Kira, but it's a business ball. So, I had to meet everyone and greet them. Each and everyone is enjoying the party. While talking with others, I glanced many times towards Kira to check whether she is doing fine. Of course, she caught everyone's attention here. And I know these greedy bastards will try to talk with her, that's why I left her with Liam.

I was with some of my business partners, talking with them in the corner of the Hall. Three of them were not paying attention to our conversation, but were glancing at other direction. I followed their gaze, it was no surp rise...they were looking at my Kira. Fucking assholes.

"She will look so good when------", they were whispering among them-selves, but I heard it. "Don't you dare complete the sentence. Shut your fucking mouths. She's mine", I gave them my best angry look.

I was furious my jaw clenched, as they talked about my woman. They are just the new businessmen...they think so high of themselves just because they work for me. Basically their boss works for me and they work under him. But I'm here from many years and have a lot of experience and not to mention the most richest businessman.

They looked scared and instantly regretted what they just said. Because everybody knows that I can end their so called business in just one moment.

"S-Sir....I.... We didn't k-knew-------", one of them started speaking but I shut him down. "I said shut your mouth. Remember if any one of you, even look at her, I will make sure to pluck your eyeballs out of you....and that's my word."Everyone stayed quiet. I made sure my voice is threatening and is only reachable within the group. I didn't wanted to disturb the whole party.

Nobody dared to look at me. I look at everyone and said, "It's not just for them but everyone of you. When I give my word, you know that I will never back down." Three of them were sweating in fear.

"I'm sorry Mr. Knight. I will make sure that I-I will punish them for their b-behaviour", their boss approched to me slowly, while stuttering. "Oh..believe me, that's not gonna happen again, because I don't want them here or in other future meetings. It's better you kick them out now!!!", I shout and left no room for them to speak.

I was so furious and angry, but when I see Kira smiling at me....it's like my whole mood is changed and a huge smile appears on my face. I decided that I will not leave Kira and stay beside her all the time. I don't care about the business partners...fuck them. Besides everyone should know that she belongs to me.

Famous models, influencers, artists were also present here. I introduced Kira to some of my trustworthy people and greeted their wifes and families. I'm so happy that I'm attending this ball with her. It feels so natural. We also danced together.

Kira is still not back yet. Fuck, I'm so obsessed with her that I can't leave her alone anymore. A part of me is also worried because she doesn't takes so much of time in washroom. Without wasting no time, I decide to check on her. I am near the washroom when I hear Kira screaming my name. Fuck!!! I immediately ran fast towards the washroom.

The moment as I enter, I see Kira against the wall. A stranger grabbed her arms and is forcing himself on her. It made my blood boil in anger. I didn't hesitate to throw a punch straight out and hit right in his face. I grab him by his shirt collar and throw more harsh and brutal punches in his face. I didn't stop. My fist is covered with his blood and his face is brutally damaged. He just passed out and I pushed him hard on the floor.

I move towards Kira. She is sitting on the floor scared and crying. I crouch down and try to calm her. She is already shaken up. "Shh... Baby, it's me", she instantly hugs me and I wrap my arms around her and calm her down. I call Liam for help. "Baby calm down, I'm here now. I'm sorry Kira. It's okay baby", I whisper in her ear. She slowly calms down.

"Ch-Charles....h-he's b-back. J-Jason I-I...", she is unable to say it properly, but I got it. I'm glad that I punched him more and he deserves it. I wipe her tears and I see red marks on her cheek. This asshole hurt her and I'm gonna make sure he pays for his mistakes. "Don't say anything baby. I'm here now", I kiss her forehead.

"What happened --------Holy Shit!!!", Liam comes closer. "Liam, just take him out of my sight. I will tell you everything later and I will also tell what to do with him. And make sure no one sees you", Liam nods. "I will call other guys and I cleared the path, you can go outside from the other way and car is parked there", I nod at him and carry Kira in my arms. "Call me when she is okay. Take care", Liam said and I got out.

Soon I reached out, the driver was ready with the car. I carried her to the backseat. "Did he hurt you anywhere?", I started checking her hands, face but she shakes her head. "Don't worry, we will go to the hospital.""N-No, I j-just want to go h-home please", she rests her head on my chest. "Okay. Take us home ?", I said to my driver. Our ride is quite. She needs me and I am gonna be there for her, just like she had been for me.

We pulled up at my house, and driver opened the door. I carried Kira in my arms and I took her to my room. I asked her, if she wanted a bath. She just nodded her head. I turned on the bath for her and undressed her and placed her in the bath. I am worried about her. She is not saying anything.

"Baby, talk to me. I'm really worried about you", I held her hands. She looks up at me, "Will you just hold me, I need you.""Of course sweetheart."

I undressed myself and sit behind her and held her in my arms. She leans her back on me and we interlock our fingers. I give her comforting kisses on her neck and shoulder. I really want her to speak to me, but she is tired. I will talk with her tomorrow. We both got out of bath and placed her in the bed. She falls asleep.

I run my hand through her hair, " I'm sorry Kira that this incident happened with you. But I promise it won't happen again", I kiss her forehead. She is deep sleep. I grab my car keys and drive to my old mansion where Liam held Charles captive. I told Liam everything and also asked him to gather some information about the fucker.

I arrive to the place. I enter the room where I see Charles tied to the chair and is still unconscious. Liam and other guards are also present in the room. "First of all, how did this fucker attended the ball?", I question Liam. "Guess what, he is dating a famous model and that's how he entered the ball."

"Anything else?", I don't want to leave him this easily. I'm controlling myself to not to kill him. "Well, this guy is never stable, he has been travelling many cities. To note down one thing is that his brother is a drug dealer and they both have done many crimes and may have connections with other criminals too. He had abused many women. Many of them reported it to the cops but he always came out. In short this guy is a fucked up asshole", Liam states and hand me a file of Charles.

"How did you gather so much information in short time?"."One of my friend is a cop and I thought I should ask him first", Liam answers. I tell him to throw water on his face to wake him up. With the splash of cold water on his face he wakes up. He looks around, I couldn't control myself anymore and I throw one more punch to his face.

"Ahh...just stop....l-leave me a-alone", he coughs. "P-Please....l-let m-me go. Please.""And he begs too", Liam adds. "You should've have thought that before hurting Kira. You will pay for that and trust me it's not going to be easy", I leave the room and Liam joins me.

We are in the garden and having some drinks. "What would happen if we kill him?", I ask Liam. "His brother is having a very bad record and I don't think after killing Charles he is going to sit quiet. We can get in problem because of that", he explains.

"I know, that's why I want to deal with this peace of shit legally. I don't want to cause anymore problems. Even if we do it legally, he will be free after few years. He should be punished for abusing women", I sigh. "We can do one thing", Liam said. "What?"."We can put more cases on him. You know....in the way he can't get out of it. You can do this because you are a powerful billionaire", he said and finishes his drink.

"How the hell do you get these ideas?", I chuckle. He shrugs in response and laughs. "Okay, let's do this way. You can handle this situation and if there is any problem you call me", Liam nods.

"There are few more hours left for the sunrise. Torture him and when all your work is done hand him to the cops.""Oh...It will my pleasure. Anyways I needed to blow of some steam", he stretches out his body." Thanks Liam. ""Just go home idiot", we both chuckle.

My one and only friend since childhood. I never heard of his parents, but mama said that his father died due to cancer and his mother was never in the picture. His grandmother worked as maid in our house and he used to come with her. Since then we used to play together. We were best friends.

After the incident happened with me and when I returned home after 6 years, I became reserved person. I learnt that his grandmother died and my family took responsibilities of him and his studies. He used to come over and talk with me but I shut him down. Years passed by I slowly used to have small conversation with him. Despite having a big distance between us he knows me better. He understood me like no one else did. He knows how to deal with me. He always supports me and stays by my side.

I know he deserved better than I treated him. I will make sure he knows that I need a friend like him in my life. He is one and only true friend for me.

I soon returned back home. I changed my clothes and placed Kira in my arms again.

I woke up rubbing my eyes, she is not there beside me. I'm panicking now. I checked my room but she was not there. I shout out her name but no response. Her phone is here, where did she go. "Stop shouting, I just went down to grab breakfast for you", she places the food on the table. She gives me a warm hug and kiss my chest.

"Laszlo, I'm ready to talk.""Hmm...okay." We sit down on the bed. "I don't know how he entered, but he grabbed me and I tried to call out your name....he slapped me", my fists clenches again. I cup the cheek where he slapped her and run my thumb back and forth. Tears are formed in her eyes and she leans into my hand.

She looks down at my hand which is currently bruised because of punching his shitty face. She places soft kisses to each one of my knuckles snd gives me a sad smile. "What happened to him?"."You don't need to worry about that. I already took care of it", I pull her close to me. I told her everything. She didn't said anything and stayed close to me.

There is a knock on the door. "Can I come in? You know....if you guys are making out I will leave", Liam bangs the door. "Why this guy always want to interrupt us?". I sigh and Kira chuckles and I said Liam to come in. He comes in with a bunch of files in his hand and take a seat in front of us.

"How are you now?", Liam asks Kira. "Much better. Thanks Liam for everything.""Please Kira, don't thank me. Well I need your signatures on these papers", he hands me the file. I read it. It's about what we talked last night. I nod at him and sign the papers. Kira looks confused but doesn't say anything. I give back the file to him.

"Here's the information about Aaliana's boyfriend", Liam hands me another file. "Laszlo!!", Kira glares at me."Baby it's for good. I need to know about this guy", I said to her and she shakes her head.

"Before you read it, your Aunt Janella manipulated her to be in a relationship", Liam said. I read his file. His name is Justin. I sigh. God, this guy is no good for Aaliana. I love my sister and I don't want anybody hurting her. I feel more bad because of what Aunt Janella is doing to her.

I get it that she's her daughter but Aaliana deserves a chance to find her love. And the way Aunt Janella controls her life, I just don't like it. "Your aunt wants Aaliana to date him because, Justin seems to be the richest heir amongst her friend circle", Liam adds. Aunt Janella is nice person but her high standards and high demands are difficult to deal with.

"I will talk with Aunt Janella", I give back the file. "No Laszlo", Kira stops me. "But Kira-----""No Laszlo. If you talk...I don't think it might end well. It's between a daughter and a mother. If someone needs to talk with your aunt, it's Aaliana herself. It's her life and her decisions."I think over what Kira said. She has a point, and I think Aaliana should stand up for herself.

"If you need to talk with someone, I think you should talk with Aaliana", Kira said. "Hey Kira, If you ever leave Jason...you know I'm always available for you", Liam winks at Kira. "Fuck off Liam", I glare at him. "Don't worry. He is already head over heels with someone I know", Kira wraps her arms around me. "Wait what!! Who is she?", I'm surprised. "Yeah whatever, I'm leaving", Liam scoffs and is ready to leave.

"Liam!!", I stop him and he turns back. "Please take care of Aaliana and look after her", he smiles and nods. He leaves, me and Kira are alone again. She buries her face in my neck and places small kisses. "Baby, Can I ask you something?", Kira places her chin on my chest and looks up at me. "You never mentioned your parents. Where are they?", she sighs and looks down.

"I didn't had good relationship with my parents", she said. "My family was not perfect. When I was 18 years old, my parents forced me to get married. But I didn't listened to them, I wanted to continue my studies", I pat her back and hug her.

"I just wanted them to support me, but they didn't.They just wanted me to get married to a rich man and when I refused they cut their ties with me", she rubs her tears away, I kissed her forehead.

"Laszlo I have a small sister. She's two years younger than me. She cried a lot when I left but I had no choice. She got married three years ago....I tired to contact her but it was no use. She's angry with me. I just hope one day she could forgive me."

"I can help you with contacting her", I said. "You know who she is married to? She's married to Dave Robinson, the CEO of RedSpace Company", she states. "What!! She is your sister. I worked with him few times....he's a good man and once he invited me for lunch. His wife...I mean your sister was very nice. But how did she end up marrying Robinson?.""I don't know. But I heard that she is happy, that's what matters. It's late Laszlo, I will turn on the bath for you", she goes to the bathroom.

I'm not angry at her parents but I pity them. They had lost a daughter who every parent would want. Robinson didn't attended the ball because of his schedules. But his PA attended the ball last night. She wants to meet her sister. Both of them are right in their own places. I promise that I will unite both of them soon.

____

I just wanted to have a quick word with you all. Thanks for showing all your support by reading this book. Because of my college, it's been difficult to update the next chapters. I am balancing both so please keep up with me. Once again thank you so much for your support.☐

Chapter - 27 - Victor

K IRA

By seeing Charles again brought up all my memories back from past. I also remembered my parents and my sister....how am I not close to anyone of them. When Jason talked about my sister Athena...I wanted to cry. I missed her more, and I know she's is angry with me. I don't know when or how I'm going to meet her....I just want my little sister back.

Days went by, Jason helped to distract me after the incident and it worked. I am switching back to normal. Jason told me about what he did to Charles. He also told me about his past crimes. I didn't said anything. I wanted Charles to get punished for destroying the life's of many women. After that incident, Jason appointed two bodyguards for me.

I know he wants to protect me, but I didn't had the habit of having two people following my back everywhere. Everyone in the hospital knows that I am dating Jason. It was published in newspapers and magazines having our photos on front page. It was weird. Whenever I entered any room, everyone starts whispering amongst themselves. I don't pay much of my attention to this. They will forget about it within short time.

Last week Jason asked me to move in with him. I was over the moon, but I wanted him to be sure. Next day itself, he literally shifted all my things in his house. We both live in the same house now. Everything is going in the right place and I hope it does the same in future too.

Only thirty minutes are left to end my shift. It's almost dinner time. I still have two more patients to check. My phone starts ringing, it's Jason"Hello, I have finished my work, I will leave in few minutes and pick you up", he said. "Yeah, that's fine. I still have patients to check. I will call you back", I hang up. I do rest of my work. Next few days are going to be tiresome for me. My team has many surgeries to perform.

I'm in the reception hall. I collected all my things. Today April is having night shift, so she is currently busy. April got mad when she knew what happened with me in the ball. But she relaxed when I told her Jason took care of it. I thought she would be sad that I was moving in with Jason, but she proved me wrong. She was happy and said that now she can have one night stands in her own room. Silly girl. She is just the female version of playboy.

Suddenly two arms wrapped me from behind and I gasped, it's Jason I can smell his scent and I know it's him. He kissed my shoulder blade and I turn around. He gives me small peck on my lips. "Are you ready to go?", Jason takes my backpack. He always carried my backpack, even when I tell him not to. "Yeah. Let's go to your house"."No baby. It's our house. How many times should I tell you this", we hold each other hands and walk outside .

"Let's go to our house and have some dinner and then sleep in our lovely bed", I tease him a little. "Don't play this game with me baby. You won't want to miss your tomorrow's shift now, would you?", I swallow a huge glup, as much as I want to continue this. But something tells me that he is not going to hold back.

"You don't want to answer now?", he laughs and tighten his hold on my waist. "You know what I'm gonna do? Once we get home, I'm gonna be buried deep inside you and pound into you mercilessly and you would be moaning my name all night", I hit his arm in response. "Be ready", I think it is the warning for me. Really, I should've shut my mouth from start. But a part of me is also excited to reach home quickly.

____

He slammed in me and my legs around him tightened. "Scream my name baby", he sucked my breasts and grabbed the other one in his hand. He slapped my breasts and the pleasure is uncontrollable.

"Yes....Laszlo! Shit...Fuck me harder!", I tell and he places my one leg on his shoulder and goes deep. "That's it baby. You are doing so good. You like it when I fuck you hard right? You will wait for me, yeah?", he said and rammed hard inside me. He suck and bite my neck, making me wince in both pain and pleasure.

"Cum for me baby", he slowed and after some few thrust, he shoot his load inside me. He buries his face in my neck. "I'm really tired", he goes to the bathroom and brings a wet towel and cleans me. He always does this. He pulls me on top of him and press a kiss on my forehead.

"You need anything?", he asks and I shake my head. "Hmm...Good night baby", I just hum and drift off to sleep in his arms.

____

Just like the daily routine, we both had breakfast together but Jason has a day off today. Unfortunately I can't take a day off because today my team is having a surgery to perform. Like always, Jason doesn't listen to me and he said he will visit me in my free time. Believe me, he is really clingy.

I just talked with patients family about her condition and when we are going to perform the surgery. Now we have a break, there's no surprise Jason is already here. "Hey baby", he gives me a hug. "Jason, it's your day off. You should be resting. It's not so necessary to come and meet me", I run my fingers through his hair.

"I was bored. I knew you wouldn't be eating anything, so I stopped by. When will your surgery begin?", he cups my right cheek. "I still have 3 hours left", I smile at him. "Plenty of time. You two can leave", he said to the two bodyguards behind me.

He takes me to the cafeteria. Everyone knows about us. And it's not a new thing for them because Jason always keeps coming, so they got used it. We had our lunch and we are in the hallway right now. He makes sure to leave me at the end of the hallway but he suddenly stopped. I look back at him, he looks so afraid. "Laszlo, what's wrong?", I go closer to him. He was fine a moment ago, what happened so suddenly?

He doesn't respond and looks scared. I place my hand on his chest and he lightly grips my hand. "Please talk to me Laszlo, what's wrong?", I ask him again. "V-Vic-Victor", he whispers, and it gets me....his father. I look back, but there are so many people around here. I follow his gaze....I see a lean and old aged man who is talking with some doctor. He was right. He was right when he said he saw his father. He was not imagining him.

"I-I....need t-to go", he steps back and walks fast. I run behind him, but he quickly rushed out of the room."Jason wait, please", I called out his name many times but he didn't stop. I couldn't keep up with him. Till I reach the reception Hall, he just disappeared. I quickly run out of the hospital. I see his car has already gone. I quickly call Julius to come down with his car keys.

He comes down and hands me his car keys. He asked me if everything was alright and I replied that I will come back soon. Jason will go back home, so I drive to his home. I really don't understand what should I do? How am I going to handle him? He looked....he looked so helpless. Last time, it didn't went well. I don't want anything happening to him nor I want to him to hurt himself.

I soon arrive home. I run towards the bedroom. I try to open the door, but it's locked. I knock it twice, thrice but Jason did not opened the door. I try to catch my breath. I'm breathing heavily. There's silence for sometime. I hear his sobs, fuck why isn't he opening the door. I try harder by twisting the knob but it doesn't work.

"Laszlo, please open the door. I'm here now.""Please", I pled him. "Baby it's alright. It's just me", I bang the door but it's no use. I want to help him but I can't. I hear loud noises coming from the room, like clashing of things. My heart is beating faster and tears formed in my eyes. I just keep banging the door nonstop and talk with him. But it's no use.

My legs give up. I sit down against the door. It's silent again. I feel him, sitting against the door from his side. "Laszlo", I whisper but he did not reply. I place my hand on the door, imagining placing my hand on his cheek. I want to comfort him so badly.

"Breathe. It's okay. You are going to be okay. Just breathe. Remind yourself of all the times in the past that you've felt this scared. And remind yourself of how much each time you made it through. Life has thrown so much at you, and despite that you've survived. Breathe and trust that you can survive this too", there is silence. I know that he is listening to me. I turn myself fully towards the door.

"I know you're going through a battle in your mind right now, but I believe in you that you will beat these demons....and I am proud, because you keep fighting. We both have been each other's backbone", tears runs down my cheeks. But I want to stay strong for him. I wipe away my tears.

"Things have not been easy for us lately. I know we'll be okay in the end and I hope you believe in that too. We will get through this, together. I love you with all my heart", I take a short pause before continuing.

"Remember when I saw some someone from my past who hurt me. You were the one who helped me. You held me in your arms, you held me every night. You supported me, you were there by my side. You are my backbone baby. It's my turn now. And by doing this, you are not being fair with me", I hear someone's footsteps from behind. It's Arlo. When he sees me sitting down on floor, he ran towards me. I see him and more tears flows.

"Kira what happened?", he crouches down at my level. I tell him everything. He knocks the door, but it was no use. "Arlo please do some_____", "Kira you should go to the hospital right now"."What!! No, I can't. I can't leave him_____"Kira listen to me, Julius called me...he said me you all have a surgery to do. He said me to check up on you. They need you Kira", I totally forgot about the surgery. Only 45 minutes are left.

"But Arlo, what about Jason? He needs me"."Kira, I know you want to help him. But believe me, he needs to be alone right now. He's scared. He needs time, and he don't want to do something that he might regret it later. Trust me, I will be here till you come home. Please", I process everything and I nod my head. I take one last glance at the door.

"Arlo, please look after and take care of him"."I will", I'm on my way towards hospital. Many thoughts are going through my mind. Why is this happening with us? Why is our past coming up again and again to destroy our happiness? This all started from the hospital. I shall get my answers at he hospital.

I splash some cold water on my face. My eyes are slightly swollen. I wear my scrub, gloves, cap and surgical mask and get ready for surgery. Julius was worried about me and was relieved when he saw me. My thoughts wander back to Jason. But right now, my focus is on my patient. It's my job. My job is to save and cure people.

It was really long surgery. It was successful. I informed their family. They are happy and relieved. I changed my clothes. I called Aaron. He picks up my call, he said Jason still didn't talked with him or opened the door.

I'm worried for him. I still need to find about Jason's father. I remember his father talking with some doctor. God, I don't know his name. But I think I saw him somewhere else too. Think Kira, think. Yes! I remember now. He is the same doctor that accompanied us during Arlo's surgery.

Why I can't remember his name? But I'm sure Julius knows him. I need to talk with him. I call him and told him to wait downstairs for me. "Julius, I need to know something important?"."Calm down. I'm not going any-where", he placed his hand on my shoulder. "Do you remember the doctors that accompanied us during Arlo's surgery?", he starts to think.

"Umm..tell me something about the specific doctor you are talking abou t?"."He has blonde hair, he's tall probably your height", I said. "I think you are talking about Dr. Nicholas. He is a neurologists, and he was present there in Arlo's surgery"."Thank you so much Julius. Do you think he is still here?"."I think so. What is happening? What are you hiding from me?"."I will tell you later. Bye", I hug him and I walk towards Dr. Nicholas cabin.

I reach his cabin and knock. He replied that I can come in. "Hello doctor. I'm Dr. Kira White. I hope I'm not Interrupting you?"."Oh...no. Please have a seat", he gesture me to have a seat. I sit down. "Tell me, how can I help you?", he adjust his glasses. "Umm...sir, I don't know how to say it but I need some information".

He nods and I proceed ahead. "You were talking with some man....in the hallway, a few hours ago. He___he's name is Victor. You know him?". I ask nervously. "Victor...umm..I don't know or have a patient name Victor", he answered. What!! I remember Jason spelled his name few hours ago. He also told me that his father name is Victor. What is happening?

"Please sir, remember a man was talking with you in the Hallway. He looked aged...he also looked skinny with white hair", I persue him more to think. "Are you talking about Wingston?", what is going on? I don't know what to say. "He was the only patient, I talked in hallway few hours ago", he said.

Is he talking about the same person that I am talking. "Can you tell me something more about him?"."Well, he is suffering from Post-traumatic amnesia. He lost all his past memories. His condition was not improving. Last month, we ran some tests on him and we got to know that he is suffering from leukemia", he explained me.

Oh my god!! This is so much to handle. He lost his past memories that means he doesn't know about about Jason or his family. "From when did he started visiting the hospital?", I question him once again. I want to know everything about this situation. "Do you know him Dr. Kira?", of course I knew he was going to ask this question to me.

"I think so. I just wanted to confirm that he's the same person", I assured him. "He started coming here from past few months. Because of severe head injury and blood loss he was suffering from PTA. And now he is treating his cancer in this same hospital but with different doctor".

Now I connected everything together. I feel so bad for Jason. The person that caused so much pain to him, forgot everything. But Jason remembers every pain his father caused him.

"Ok. Thank you Doctor", I leave his cabin.

I drive back home to Jason. I don't understand how to say this to Jason. He is not even listening to me. I need to be patient with him. I reached home. I can only pray things go well with both of us.

Chapter - 28 - A Normal Life

JASON

Why is this happening with me again and again? Why I'm seeing him after all this years, and yet I get scared when I see him. I just feel like I'm nine years old boy again. He terrifies me. Like a coward I ran from the hospital. Kira was running behind me but I just ran out. I am feeling so weak. Everything was going fine....but everything gets messed up.

I locked my room. My head was exploding with all the painful memories. I can't forget those memories or his face, they still haunt me. I throw things off the table. I hit my head with my hand to stop this pain. There's banging on the door but I ignore it. I pull my hair in frustation. There's pain, frustation, tears and saddness. I collapse down on floor. There's a soft voice calling out my name and it calms me down.

It's Kira's voice. The person who I don't want to lose at any cost. I want to open the door, hug her and cry out....but I won't. I don't know what will happen if she enters the room in this state. My mind is currently filled with so many things. I don't want to hurt her anyway. I almost lost her once but

I'm not gonna lose her again. Right now, I think it's better if I'm alone sometime. I'm sorry baby.

I hear Arlo's voice...he's here. He tells Kira to go to the hospital. She has a surgery to perform. At first she was hesitant but Arlo convinced her to go.

"Hey bro, you alright?", Arlo asked me. "I don't know. I need some time alone", I bury my face in my hands. "You're not alone. Open the door and let's talk about it, or I can call Mama?.""No Arlo. I need some time.""Take your time, but don't forget that we'll are here for you. Call me if you need anything."

I calm myself down without any thoughts in my mind. Kira will come home tonight and I need to talk to her about it. She cried because of me. I will talk to her when she comes home.

I washed my face with water. I cleaned the mess in the room which was made by me. I unlock the door. I walk in my garden to get some fresh air.

She is late today. This gives me more time to think of how I am going to talk with her. I hear the sound of the car, she is home. I take few deep breaths. I hear her footsteps near the door. She slowly opens the door and I see her.

Her face is a bit down. The glow she had in her face was disappeared. By seeing her face I know she cried for me. Her eyes became moist when she saw me. She stood there in silence, I slowly approach towards her. We were few inches apart. "Baby-----In a split second she clashes with my body. She hugs me as if it was our last time. She cries her heart out.

Fuck, I feel so guilty for what I did. I hold her more close to me and rub her back. "I...I-I was so worried about y-you. Don't you d-dare do that a-again or I swear I will kick your ass.""I'm sorry Kira. I-I just needed sometime I didn't wanted to hurt you. I'm sorry", she cups my cheeks in her hands and starts kissing my face and holds me tight in her arms.

I just thought about myself, god I was so selfish. She held me in her arms like she needed comfort from me, just like I needed from her.

"Did you had your dinner?", she asks me. I shake my head. She unwraps her arms around me and takes off her coat. "Wait here, I will make something for you hmm", ahe was ready to leave, but I follow behind her and grab her hand. "Let's make it together", I kiss her palm. She gives me her cute smile.

I helped her with slicing some vegetables. I sit on the barstool in front of her. I watch her while she is cooking. She manages everything so perfectly. But I can sense something is wrong. She didn't talked much and she's in her own thoughts. I think it's because of what happened today.

We both had our dinner. I'm resting on bed with my back against the headboard and waiting for Kira. She's been in the bathroom for quite a long time. I hear the door open and she comes out in her nightgown. Why she has to look so hot in that. I'm so caught up with my thoughts that I didn't realize that she is beside me and placed her hand on mine.

"Jason, I need to tell you something?", she seems nervous. "Me too.You go first.""Jason....before I left the hospital I met someone", I didn't interrupt her, and wanted her to complete. "Jason....I got some information regarding you're fa--- I mean Victor. It seems that he has lost his memory". How does she knows about this?

"Kira, w-what are you s-saying", my voice cracks. "Jason, after my surgery________", she tells me everything, how she met the doctor. Everything seems unreal. I don't know what to say. "Jason talk to me. How do you feel?", my girl asks me.

"I-I don't know. The man who caused so much pain in my life, the man who destroyed my childhood, the man whom I don't want to see in my lifetime is b-back again. He just forgets everything like...like nothing just happened. But I remember everything even if I try to forget. It's like I'm being punished. I don't know what to do about it", I'm completely shaken. I drop my head in Kira's neck.

"You showed me that I was important, that there's a reason I'm here. You made me feel like the world was lucky to have me. And I don't know if anyone will ever make me feel that way again Kira. I'm sorry for being so weak. I always let you down. I'm trying so hard but everything seems to go wrong."

"Hey, I'm here with you, that's all matters. We're doing this together. We're going to face every problems together hmm", I just nod my head. "Jason what are you going to do about Victor, because it won't be last time you will see him", she cups my cheek.

"Honestly I don't want to do anything. I don't want to get involved in his life again. After so many years, my life is going in the right path. Not only he hurt me but also my family. My family forgot about his existence and they're happy now. I have you. I don't want to go again in the past. I believe in God, let him decide what to do with him. I want a normal life", I sigh.

"Come here", I lay my head on her chest and she massages my head. "It's been a long day. You need to rest. You have work tomorrow", she kisses my forehead. I fall in sleep in her arms.

———————————

It's been few days and I'm feeling a lot better. I feel fresh. Yesterday was my last therapy session. Doctor was glad with my improvement.

Kira is at work and I'm in my office right now. Today I'm also meeting Mama. My office door opens, "Hello Brother. It's good to see you", Aaliana enters the room and takes a seat in front of me. "How many times do I have to tell you before you enter, knock the door", I totally forgot that I called Aaliana to meet me when she was free.

"I'm sorry. I don't take orders, I barely take suggestions", she replied. "B rat.""I've been called worse.""Ok enough. First of all I called you here to have a good brother and sister bonding", I fold my hands. "Thank you very much for thinking about me. Bye!", she gets up from her seat and is ready to leave.

"Ana I'm serious.""Fineee, but be fast. I don't want to miss my cheerleading practice", I examine her face and I can say that she is really exhausted. "Where have you been these days? Mama said you barely even come ho me.""Liam didn't tell you anything? Because I always find his nose in my business."

I take a deep breath. God, everytime this girl tests my fucking patience. "He did. But I want to hear it from you. So answer the damn question", I glare at her. "I've....I've been trying new things, and you know that I've a boyfriend now."

I know Aaliana, she's brilliant in her studies and she loves ballet but Aunt Janella didn't allowed her to continue. I also know that she's the one that's forcing her to try something new and the stupid boyfriend thing.

"I believe cheerleading is one of them?"."Yes", she looks down. "I know Aunt Janella has forced you into this and other things. I know she is reason behind your so called boyfriend thing. But are you really happy with this?".She didn't said anything. She is confused. It seemed like she was battling with herself.

"I wish my life would be different. Mom has different plans for me. I am following her as she says....but it feels like I'm betraying myself by being a different person. I don't want to let her down, but at the same time I don't know how to tell her. You know right, how she is, she wants everything to be perfect", she drops her head on the table.

"Don't wish for it, work for it. It's your life. You're the only one who can change it. You are still young and you have plenty of time. Whatever decision you will make, I'm always on your side", she smiles at me. "I never thought I would be discussing this with you", she laughs. We both get up. I go to her and give her a hug.

"Ana, Liam cares for you. So try to stop being a bitch towards him", she hits my chest. "I will try but it's so fun to piss him off. You should see his face", we both laugh. "Take care. Love you ", she kissed my cheek and leaves. She is really something else. I really feel bad for her future husband. Poor guy, he is going to experience hell with her. I chuckle.

————————

I complete my work. I'm going to meet Mama. It's been a long time since we spent some time together. I need to discuss so many things with her. My phone rings.....it is Kira. I pick up my call. "Hello babe. Did you finished your work?"."I finished it just now. You are a having a break?"."Yep. I'm so bored", she says in a weary tone.

"You know....last night I fantasized about sitting on your face", she whispered. Shit, my dick almost jerked in its place. "I wish I could have you right now, at this very instant", she speaks in a seductive way. "Fuck baby, I'm so hard right now", I breathe out. "I also keep thinking about you grabbing me and having your way with me", her voice got more low and slow. Is she trying to kill me?

"Tell me how badly you want me to fuck you. I already know you're wet down there", I remove buttons on my pants. I close my eyes. I imagine her riding on top of me. She moans my name again and again while I take one of her nipple in my mouth and grab the other one in my hand.

Fuck, I think my dick is gonna burst anytime. I'm really frustrated that my girl is not with me right now, and like a damn vixen, she is teasing me mercilessly.

I hear her laugh on the phone. "Baby, do you think this is funny?", I'm so frustrated now. "I didn't knew you would get horny so easily. Maybe I should keep doing this to you", she giggles. "You're the only woman who makes me lose it like this", I breathe out.

"So help me with this. It's your fault my dick is so hard", I groan. "I don't think so, I need to go back to my shift. Like now", she teases me again. "Oh no. Don't you dare baby. You're going to forget your name after I'm done fucking you tonight."

"Hmm...I would like that. But first jerk it off by yourself and imagine me doing it.""Just wait until we reach home. Tonight you are not allowed to cum until I say so"."Bye babe", she hangs up on me. She's in so much trouble tonight.

I sigh and look down. Hell, I need to take care of this before I go out. I swear, I'm gonna punish her tonight.

"I hope I don't see Victor", Mama rests her head on my shoulder, while we sat on the swing in our garden.

"I erased that man from my life many years ago. I wanted to destroy him. I fought with him and in that process I lost you. I feel like....this incident started with me. I'm sorry Jason. I didn't protected you from him. I saw you in so much pain and yet I couldn't do anything. I lost you and I constantly blamed myself for it. Because of that I didn't paid much attention to Arlo and was not able to take care of Liam, he was my responsibility. I think I failed as a mother", tears falls down from her eyes on my shoulder.

"You don't need to blame yourself nor you have to apologize, it was not your fault. You were broken when you caught Victor cheating on you. You were strong, you fought for us. You did so much for our family.You gave me life, nurtured me, held me and loved me unconditionally. Thanks for always being there for me when I needed you.You also took care of Liam like your own child and he loves you too Mama", I placed a kiss on her forehead.

My mother went through really hard times and cried herself to sleep, but she faced every difficulties and raised us. "Mama?"."Hmm"."I'm thinking that I should settle down.""You already are. You have a job, your family and a girlf--------Oh my God!!!",She gasps and covers her mouth with her hand. I laugh when I see her surprised.

"I'm going to propose Kira. I want to marry her Mama, I am hoping for your blessing", once again her eyes became moist. "Goodness! My baby boy is getting married. I'm so happy today. You have my blessing. It's impossible to get a perfect daughter-in-law like Kira", I wipe away her tears and a small laugh comes out of my lips.

"Mama, I didn't propsed her yet", she hits my shoulder. "Shut up son. I know she will say yes", she smiles. I hope so.

"So, what's your plan?", she sniffs her nose. "Umm...I didn't fully planned it yet. I might need your help."We talked for hours. Mama gave me really good ideas for the proposal. A part of me is excited and also a part of me is nervous. We will be starting a new chapter in our lives.

———————

I want to go home but I planned to meet someone in the restaurant. I hope she comes.I can't believe I planned to meet everyone today. I arrived early and wait for her. I hear the sound of heels, I look straight in front of me------- she's here.

"Hello Mr. Knight."

———————————

Hii guys.I hope y'all are doing well. It's been a long time and I know you all are mad at me.My friend passed away 2 months ago. It was a very difficult time for me.I'm sorry that I kept y'all waiting and didn't update further chapters. Friends, please take care of your health and your loved ones. Thank you everyone for your support☐Cheers to the New Year! Cheers to a year filled with abundant love, fun, and excellent physical health!☐

———————————

Only few chapters are left to complete the story. Do you guys think I should write a story on Liam and Aaliana. If you guys are interested please let me know in the comments.

Chapter - 29 - Be Mine Forever

KIRA

I keep some files in my wardrobe. Jason has not returned home yet. He said he would be meeting his mother. I'm glad that they are spending some time together. Jason needed it. Thinking of Jason, I remember how I teased him on phone call earlier today. I smile remembering how he was sexually frustrated.

I remember, how he said that he would punish me for teasing him. God! When will he come home. He should be home now. My phone rings, it's Julius.

"Hey Kira.""It's been only two hours since we left. What happened?.""R elax. I just want the files from today. Send me those files right now.""Are you kidding me! If you needed it, why did you gave it to me."

"Kira----"Fine, I will share images on phone.""So, how was your dinner?", he asked me. "What do you mean?.""I was passing by the restaurant where

I saw you and Jason. I couldn't see your face because your back was faced to me.''I came directly to home, I didn't stop by anywhere.

"Umm....Julius I didn't went to any restaurant after work.""Oh! I thought that was you. It must be someone else."

Now hold up! Jason was with a woman. He said that he was only going to meet his mother. He would've told me if he was going to meet a woman. He never meets someone outside other than his office. Ok, I'm overthinking. She must be his business partner.

"Hey you there", Julius speaks. "Yeah. She--she must be his business partner. I will send those files", I hang up.

I hear the car sound, Laszlo must be home. I look at him, he is exhausted and tired. But when he sees me, a smile appears on his face. He leaves his bag on table and lifts me up. I giggle when he kisses my neck.

"Laszlo, put me down", he ignores what I said and doesn't stop smothering my face in kisses. He walks towards the sofa with me in his arms. I wrap my legs around his waist. He sits on the sofa with me in his lap. He drops his head in my neck and continues to torture me with his kisses. He stops and takes a deep breath in my neck.

"You smell so sweet baby", he grips my waist tightly. "You ate something?", he stucks few strands of my hair behind my ear. "Yes, as you ate in the restaurant", he looks confused. "Umm...how do you know?.""Julius told me that he saw you in the restaurant......with a woman", I whisper the last part.

"Oh.....so you have your spy on me huh", he kisses my shoulder blade. "Yes. Now, who was she Laszlo? I remember you said you don't meet anyone outside", I know I sound jealous...fuck it I am jealous.

"Where to start. Let's start by telling you that her husband is my long old business partner. We decided to meet for a project, but he got sick so his wife came. That's it. Pure Business ", he grins. Oh that's why he met her.

"Were you jealous? I mean this is new for me you know. You getting jealous", he chuckles. "I'm not. I was just curious", I lied.

"Hmm...Liar. You are behaving like a bad girl. You tease me, had a dirty talk on phone with me, and now you are lying. That's not what good girls do", he tightens his hold on my waist with one hand and lightly tweaks my nipple with other hand.

"No Lasz-----"Shh...baby. Did you really think I would forget that? You've been a naughty girl. You need to be punished", he gets up from the sofa and lifts me over his shoulder.

"Laszlo don't you d------"Careful baby. Anything you say will get you in a lot of trouble than this", by saying this he spank my ass and I gasp.

"Remember everything I said? Tonight I won't be going easy on you. I'm going to show you, how I felt at that time."

He walks straight to our room. He throws me in bed. Jason stood in front of me. He wasted no time and removed his suit and pants. He climbs over me and clash his lips with mine. Giving him more, I slightly part my lips and his tongue instantly slides inside. He bites my lips roughly. The kiss is wild and rough.

He undressed me and grabs my breasts and pushed me down on bed. He starts to suck my neck and twisting my hard nipples. "Laszlo", I moan. In response he sucks even harder. "You've been a naughty girl and I need to punish you", he got up and went to his closet and he brings handcuffs with him.

"Ready baby?", I slowly nod at him. "Words love", he lights kiss my cheek and whispers. "Yes Laszlo", I smile at him and peck his lips. "That's not gonna work now", he laughs. He pulls my hands above my head and handcuffs me to the bed.

My heart is beating so fast. This is new side to me. He senses that I am a little uncomfortable. "Hey, if you feel uncomfortable, I will remove it", I want to explore everything with him. I trust him. I shake my head and he pecks my lips. He pulls down my panties, reveling my wet pussy.

He spreads my thighs and moves between them. He strokes my thighs and moves his hand towards my pussy. He cups my core.

"Laszlo....", I throw my head back. "You are so wet baby", he slowly massaged my clit. With his index finger he teased me. "Please.....", my hands being cuffed to bed and the way he was teasing.....is a torture for me.

He parts my folds and slowly he slides his finger in. "Please....", I moan. "Do you want me to eat your pussy baby?", he keeps fingering me."Y-Yes please", he grins as I am completely at his mercy.

He lowers his head I can feel his breath on my core. "You are fucking beautiful baby", he places my leg above his shoulder and his head between my thighs. He started trailing kisses on inner thigh. I feel his wet kisses between them. I just can't wait. I want him to eat me out.

He latches his mouth on my core. I feel his tongue moving up and down making me gasp. I want to touch him but I can't. My moans are loud. He sucks hard and add his fingers inside me giving me more pleasure. "Don't s-stop", I moan louder and he sucks hard and fast.

I feel his finger curve inside, brusting me with even more pleasure. If he keeps doing this, I don't think I can hold it anymore. I am on the edge.....but that's when he stop and denies my release.

"Please don't do that to me", he grins down at me. He lightly slaps one of my breast. "This is exactly what I felt when you were teasing me baby", he smiles widely.

"I'm sorry, I was just messing with you."I'm frustrated. I want him. I try to fight with the handcuffs but it's no use. He removes his boxers. He is fully naked too. He is hard. Sometimes I can't believe that this thing goes inside of me.

He keeps his hand on his cock, and slowly rubs it. Fuck, this is pure torture. "Laszlo, please let me touch you", he gives me his evil smile. He is having fun watching me in this state. But I can't help. Watching him with his perfect body, perfect eight packs and his v-line. He is just so perfect.

"What do you want me to do?", he completely ignored my request. He brings the tip of his cock to my entrance. "I--I want you to fuck me", I was never this needy. No one but only Jason can do this to me. "What my baby wants, she gets it", with that he slams in his length inside me.

He is on top of me and thrusts his cock in and out of me. Instantly I wrap my legs around hs waist. I scream his name loudly and he maintains his speed. He grabs my breasts, he kisses it, sucks it and bites it. He makes sure to mark my body.

He looks at me and uncuffs me. Finally! I grab him by his neck and kiss him hard. My hands roam around his body, he fasten his speed and he swallows all my moans.

His one hand goes down to my pussy and he massages my clit, while fuck-ing me. It brings me more pleasure and brings me more to edge. "Laszlo I can't----------"No you will. You are gonna wait for me."

His voice was hard and kept thrusting in me. "Let me----------"No, I'm still not finished", he denied. I cried out with more pleasure. But I couldn't hold it anymore. I dig my nails on his back. Tears form in my eyes because of the intense pleasure.

"Let it go.....cum for me baby", that's it and I came down hard. "Fuck baby....", he grunts. I feel his cum released inside me. I run my hand in his hair. He takes my wrist and slowly massages it.

"You should pull out now", I chuckle softly. "I'm still not done with you", he glares at me. "Laszlo", I smile thinking that he is playing with me, but he thrust inside of me again. "Fuck", I moan out. "When I said I'm gonna keep you all night....it means that I'm gonna fuck you all night", he speaks in a low threatening voice sending shivers down my spine.

———————————

"Laszlo, we are gonna be late", Jason keeps on kissing my neck. We are attending some party at his family's house. He was ready and was waiting for me. I got ready with the dress he gave me. From the moment he saw me, he has not left me and keeps on smothering me with his kisses.

"Hmm...It's not my fault. You are looking so fucking beautiful", he says between the kisses. "I'm still sore down there. I barely slept last night and it took me time to get ready because I was covering all the marks on my neck", I fix his shirt collar.

"That's what you get when you tease me. But I took care of you", he winks at me. That's true. He carried me in his arms the whole day. He gave me a good body massage, a hot water bath and even cooked delicious food for me.

"Thank you", I peck his lips. "You don't need to thank me baby. I love taking care of you.I will do it for my whole life", he kissed my cheek. "Let's go Julia must be waiting for us", I hold his hand.

We arrive at his family's house. I see some new people. On our way to meet Julia we greet some guest and Jason introduces me to them. I don't even know what's the special occasion for. Finally we spot Julia with Arlo and Julius. We greet them.

"Hello Mama", Jason kissed Julia's cheek. "It's good to see you Julia", we hug each other. "Me too, darling."

"You are looking so hot today Kira", Arlo winks at me...pissing off Jason. "Fuck off, bitch", Jason glares at Arlo and he slides his arm around my waist in possesive way.

"Just kidding bro. I have my hot guy here",Julia rolls her eyes at Arlo's behavior. Arlo holds Julius's hand. I see Julius cheeks turn red. They are so cute.

"Missed me?", Aaliana comes up and puts her arm on my shoulder. "Who are you by the way", Arlo comments. "Holy Shit! You don't know me! This must be starting signs of old age", we laugh. This girl is really something else.

Arlo was going to respond her but Julia interrupted him, "Julius, why don't you both go and check on grandfather and see what he needs?.""Of course Julia", Julius drags Arlo with him. "Gosh! He is going to show hell to me in coming days", Julia says.

"Hey Jason! I need some help regarding the security", Liam joins us. He is in his usual uniform. He smiles at me and I respond the same.

"My little baby boy, there you are.....always working", Julia pulls Liam for a hug. "Little", Aaliana mocks Liam and we hide our smiles. Liam glares at Aaliana.

Julia smiles and fix Liam's collar and his hair. He just smiles down at her sweetly. It feels good to see the relationship between Julia and Liam. They don't have a blood relation, yet they hold so much love for each other. I wish my parents showed some love for me.

"It's okay mom. Just few things to take care of", Liam said. "No. You didn't eat anything today. I'm going to feed both of you. Come on", she grabs both Jason and Liam with her. They both sigh. It is funny to watch the huge men dragged by their mother, as if they are still small kids.

I see Aaliana beside me, who is busy watching Liam. "He is handsome, right?.""Yes-------I mean....what---who are you talking about?". I see her cheeks turn red. I laugh at her. "It's okay, your secret is safe with me.""No way. I don't like him. I need to go", she runs away hiding her face. They both like each other but why they are in denial.

By the time I interact with some other people. "Hey Kira, Jason is calling you. He is waiting for you in the backyard", Arlo comes up to me. I nod at him. I am on my way to meet Jason. The backyard is pitch dark. God, is he gonna kill me?

I see a ray of light and follow it. It is path and is filled with some petals and only the path had small lights. I slowly follow it. I call out his name, but there was no response. I can see Jason standing with a smile oh his face. Did he planned a dinner for us?

"Laszlo what is this?", he slowly gets down on his one kneen with a small box in his hand and he opens it.....it has a beautiful diamond ring.

"Kira White, I love you. The moment I first laid my eyes on you, I knew in my heart that my life's about to change. You are my backbone.You helped me in every way.You motivated me. I feel so happy, we have come this far. We've been through lot of difficulties. I remember how you always held me at night, protecting me. I love everything about you. I know there will be tough times but we'll go through that together", he paused. His eyes were moist. Tears already ran from my eyes.

"I checked what your name means. Kira-----It means Light. You brought light in my dark world and Regina means Queen. Of course you are my queen. I want to be with you for rest of my life. I want to experience everything the good, the bad but only with you. I love you so much. Kira Regina White will you marry me? Be my wife, be mine forever?", I try to contain the tears.

"Yes. I will marry you. I want to be yours forever", I lean down and cup his cheeks in my hand. I watch tears fall down from Jason's eyes. He slides the beautiful ring on my finger and brings his lips to mine. The kiss is passionate and filled with love. We rest our forehead against each other.

I suddenly hear clapping sound and lights on. I watch everyone was cheering for us. I can see April in the crowd. "This was not any casual party right?", he nods. "I invited them. They are here for us. I love you so mch baby", he kissed my cheek. "I love you too. So much", I said.

Everyone congratulated us on our way. Jason didn't miss a single chance to kiss me again and again.

"I have one more surprise for you", he whispers in my ear. I bring my hands around his neck. "Tell me.""Look behind", I smile. I gasp when I see what's behind me. Tears form in my eyes again.

"Hii Bookworm----------

Hey guys I am on a holiday....I need some time to fresh up my mind. So the next update will be late. Thanks for your love and support.

Chapter - 30 - Angel

J ASON

I'm so happy right now. She said yes. We are gonna get married. Everything went according to the plan I made. We are going to make new memories and I'm so excited for it.

I have one more surprise for her. "Look behind", I said to her. She smiles and turns around and gasps when she sees who is standing front of her. "Hii Bookworm."

"Ke---Kelly", Kira slowly goes near her. "Hey sis, you missed me? I certainly did", her sister's eyes are moist too. They both are in shock and staring at each otherI didn't want to interrupt them, so I kept quiet.

"Y-You----I---I---You are really here?", Kira voice cracks. Tears runs down from Kelly's eyes and she just nods. The next moment they both are hugging each other and crying.

I know Kira missed her sister. She is her only family. On this special occasion I didn't want her to miss out anything. I will do anything for her, if it means to unite her with her sister.

"I-I'm sorry Kelly, I didn't w-wanted to leave you. I am sorry", Kelly wipes away Kira's tears. "I should've known that you were going through so much. I just wanted to be with my sister", she sniffs.

"You are grown up...Oh my god! You are married now", they both laugh. "How did you do it?", Kira looks at me. "You remember when I said I met someone in the restaurant, it was her actually."

I want Kira to be happy. She told me everything about her sister. Luckly her husband and I are good business partners. By the connections I somehow got Kelly's number. I called her and explained her everything. First she didn't agreed at all, but after trying to convince her she decided to meet me. I texted her the details and hope that she comes.

I never did like this in my life, like calling and requesting them to meet. But for my Kira I will do anything.

I hear the sound of heels and look front. I see Kelly. Thank god, she is here. "Hello Mr. Knight", she greeted me. "Hello Mrs Robinson, please take a seat", she is younger than me, but still she is so intimidating. She and Kira share some familiar features, same face structure, almost same height except their eye colour. Her are black well my Kira's eyes are brown.

The waiter brings the dinner. "I ordered some food, you can order anything you like.""No it's fine", she smiles.

"I will not beat around the bush. As you know your sister is my girlfriend. She misses you a lot. You are the only person she has as a family. I know that you are sad and angry with what she did, but she had her reasons. Give her a chance to explain herself", I finished saying.

She took some seconds, "Does she knows that you are meeting with me?" ."No.""We both had a good bond. We both were there for each other. But suddenly she leaves me with our parents, who never cared for anyone of us. There were so many times I needed her, but she was not there. I fought alone and now...I would like to be alone."

"You are right, she was not there for you. She would've taken you with her, but she didn't wanted you to suffer because of her. She hides all her problems behind a smile. Behind her smile was pain and hurt. She just wanted to protect you", I sigh.

"I know you miss her too. I'm not asking you to forgive her, just give her a chance. Be with her. You both need each other."

"My sister really does have a effect on you", she smiles. "You have no idea", I chuckle. "Call me Kelly. You really sound as I am older than you.""Okay Kelly.""So, you become my brother in law right?.""Ohh...about that actually-----------

---

"So that's how I planned everything.""You did this for me. Thank you. I love you", she comes and hugs me. "I didn't wanted anything to be left out. How can I forget about your sister", I kiss her forehead.

"Hey, I still didn't forgive you fully", Kelly said. They both laugh. Everyone congratulated us. Mama was so happy that she started crying. Grandpa was proud of me.

There is slow music and some couples are dancing. "Shall we?", I ask Kira, she nods and smiles at me. We slowly dance with our bodies slowly swaying with the music. She rests her head on my chest.

"Thank you for everything. Thanks for coming into my life. Thanks for bringing peace in my life. I love you Laszlo", she kisses me.

The night was one of my best memories with Kira and my family. We reached home late night. Kira was tired, she slept the moment when she rested on the bed. I kissed her forehead and slept beside her.

Few days later Kira told me that my father Victor commited suicide. It was also published in newspapers. I didn't know how to express this, but I felt relieved. There was no looking back at my past...it was long gone. It's time to live up my present and create a better future for my family.

———————————————

Today Kira's shift is going to end early. So we thought it would be good to spend some time strolling in the park. As usual there were many people in the park. Kira holds my hand and we both stroll in the park. She talked about how her day went and about her sister. We recently had dinner with Kelly and her husband.

She continues to talk and I look front, I see a small girl sitting on the bench. I saw her somewhere. I think harder.....I remember, I met her in the park. Ella....Angel.

"Angel!!!", I shout at her."Where?", Kira looks around. "There", I point at the small girl and I grab Kira's hand and run towards her.

Ella looked confused and looked everywhere. But when she saw me, a big smile appears on her face. I crouch down and she hugs me. After so many months, I finally meet her. I kiss her head.

"Mr. Teddy bear", she pinches my cheeks and laughs. "You remember me?", she nods at me. I am happy that she didn't forget me. "Ella. My angel", she giggles. Ella looks behind me and looks at Kira. Kira is surprised.

"Kira meet Ella. Ella meet my girlfriend Kira", Kira also bends down. "She's pretty", Ella touches her hair."Thanks, Ella you are beautiful too. Just like an Angel.""She is an angel", I said and Ella giggles again.

I explained Kira how Ella and I met. It's been quite some time. "It's late. Bye Mr. Teddy bear, bye Miss Kira. Will you come tomorrow?", Ella asked me. "Sure, we will", she smiles and runs fast.

"I didn't know you were so good with kids", Kira holds my hand. "We promised her that we will come tomorrow, so remember that", Kira said. "I won't forget."

____

Three of us sit on the bench. Ella is sitting on my lap, hugging me closely. "She really likes you", Kira runs her hand through Ella's hair. "I like him too", I chuckle.

We were talking I see some red marks on her neck. Yesterday there were no marks. I remove aside some of her hair to see closely. It's a grab mark. I get panic.

"Angel----who did this?." I know they are not accident marks. I am very much familiar with abused marks. Fuck, someone is abusing her. "Nothing", she hides her face in my chest.

"Angel don't lie to me. Tell me Ella", I lift her face slightly. She is crying and she continuously shakes her head.

"Let me see", Kira tries to see it but Ella hugs me close, as if Kira is going to hurt her. "It's okay Angel. She's not going to hurt you", she cries hugging me. I try to calm her down.

After few minutes she stops crying. I wipe away her tears and clean her face with my handkerchief. Her eyes are red. "Angel someone's hurting you? You can tell me. I promise I will help you", she looks at me and takes her time and nods her head.

"Who?", she shakes her head again. Fuck, she is so scared. "Trust me Ella", she sniffs her nose. "M-My mo-mother." That's it. I stand up with Ella in my arms.

"We need to do something.""Calm down Jason. First we need to think."I am not able to think anything. How can her mother hurt her?

"We can't do it ourselves. We need to know everything. If...If she is having bruises?", Kira said. Kira tries to see but Ella doesn't allow her. "She trusts you Jason. First, let's get out of here", I nod at her. Ella is rambling something but I can't hear exactly what she is saying.

We enter our car. She is still in my arms. I ask her again if her mother hurts her often, she nods her head. I see some bruises on here back too."I will contact ChildHelp Services", Kira contacts them.

I was suffering the same in the past but no one helped me back then. But I'm gonna help her. I ask Ella where her house is and she directs us. The colony she lived in is good. How did nobody noticed this?

We were two blocks away from her house. We waited for the cops and the ChildHelp Agency. Soon they arrived. We discussed everything with them. We showed them her bruises to them. Later we got to know that Ella had bruises on her chest too. Some were old. We waited outside the house.

The cops and the other members went inside the house. After some time they came out with a woman. The cops arrested her. The woman looked high on drugs. She saw Ella in my arms.

"I should have chained this bitch and never let her out", she shouts and curses at us. Ella gets scared and hides her face. I'm so glad we got to know early about this. We would've never know what this woman might have done to her.

I take Ella a little aside from her house. Kira is talking with the ChildHelp Agency. She comes to me. "They said that they will investigate about her mother further. They said that they will help Ella with her health and look after her", Kira said.

I want to look after Ella. I don't want to let her go after all this. I need some time with her. "But--------"I explained them that she is not in the right state. I told them I am a doctor so they agreed. They said they will pick her up tomorrow. I'm worried about her", Kira holds Ella's hand. "Thank you Kira."

We reach home. I'm so happy Ella is coming home with us. We had some dinner together. Ella didn't eat much, she was quite. Kira gave her a bath and treated her bruises. I tucked her to our bed. She falls asleep.

"She is beautiful", Kira said. Ella is sleeping between me and Kira. "I'm happy she's here with us", I said. "Me too."

I woke up alone in bed. I think Kira and Ella are downstairs. I freshup and go down. I hear giggling sounds from kitchen. I see Kira and Ella cooking pancakes. Ella is sitting on kitchen counter and Kira is making pancakes. It is such a beautiful sight to see them together.

"Good morning girls", I kiss their forehead. "We are making pancakes", Ella said. "Ella woke up early. We decided to make breakfast", Kira pecks my lips. "Hmm...I like pancakes", I tickle Ella and she laughs. Kira and I join her too.

"She was a little hesitant, but she gave in", Kira said looking at Ella, who was busy drawing something. We hear a knock on the door. Kira goes to open. I look at Ella.....having her for only few hours made us do happy, she deserves a good childhood.

Kira's face was down and mine as well when I saw the agency members from yesterday. They came for Ella. Ella sees them, and runs to me and hide behind my legs. They are discussing something with Kira and remove some papers from their bag.

"I d-don't want t-to go", Ella whispers and she holds my hand tightly. "Ella we have new toys with us. Will you come with us and see them?", one of them said and Ella shakes her head. "Ella you will have new friends there", Ella doesn't listen to them and runs upstairs.

I go behind her. She went to my bedroom. I see her sitting in the corner of the bedroom. She is crying again. I slowly go towards her.

"I d-don't.....don't", she is crying so hard that she is not able to complete. "I w-will....I will b-be a good girl", my heart breaks seeing her and pleading to me.

"Calm down angel. I will not let you go. Shh....come here", I open my arms and she accepts it. Kira is still down with them. I don't know how to explain this to her but I don't want to let go Ella.

Ella clutches my shirt tightly and I kiss her head. Slowly the door opens and Kira comes in and she sees us. She comes and sit down with us. She plays with Ella's hair. I need to tell her. "Laszlo can we adopt Ella?", my eyes widened and I'm surprised.

"I wanted to ask the same thing", she smiles at me. "I know it's too early for us. I didn't got the love from my parents but I want to give it to her. I don't know anything about being a parent but I know we can do this together", she rests her head on my shoulder and watches at Ella.

Ella looks at us. She is confused. "Smile now angel, you're not going any-where. You are staying with us here, forever angel", I kiss all over her face and open my arms for Kira. She joins me and tickles Ella making her laugh.

It's true that things didn't go as they are planned but I'm so much grateful it turned out to be so much better. Now I have my Kira with me and also a beautiful Angel. I couldn't ask for more.

chapter. Love you guys □

Chapter - 31 - A New Beginning....

KIRA

I have become a parent now. I have a new responsibility to take care of Ella. I love her so much. It is a new kind of feeling. Everyone was surprised. Within few days after Jason's proposal, we adopted Ella. Jason's family didn't had any problem with it. Julia was happy and she already taught Ella to call her grandmother.

The agency members were downstairs. We told them that we want to adopt Ella and they didn't have problem with our decision. We got the adoption papers and we are her new parents. Honestly I don't know anything about being a mother.

Ella has a very good bond with Jason. Jason was over the moon when Ella called him Papa. I was happy for him but I wanted Ella to call me Mama too. But with me it's a little difficult. She still seems to have a little problem to open up to me. I felt really sad that she hasn't fully trusted me yet.

It's because of her ex-stepmother. Yes step mother. The cops told us that Kira's biological mother died giving birth to her. Ella's biological father had a second marriage. He died due to brain tumor, and from there her ex-stepmother started abusing her. That's the reason she a bit distant with me. But I will keep on trying and I know that one day Ella and I will have a good relation.

I taught it would be better if Ella attends some therapy and Consulling sessions. Parenting is really a difficult job. Both me and Jason changed our schedules. We both wanted to give more time to Ella.

Sometimes she would have nightmares. We took care of her health. We admissioned her to new school, her extra activity classes. I am really proud of Jason, he takes care of her, loves her and plays with her. He has grown so much.

My phone rings and I pick up."Kira are you ready? I will come to pick you up in 10 minutes". Oh no fuck. I totally forgot that today Ella is giving her speech. Today all students are going to give speech in front of all parents.

"Yes. I will be ready". I hang up. I quickly pack my things. I can't be late. I don't want to miss Ella's speech. I'm ready in time. Soon, Jason arrives with car, we both head towards her school.

"I'm excited to hear her speech", Jason said holding my hand. "Me too", I fix his collar and his tie. He kisses my forehead. We reach her school. There is no surprise that we are in the front row with the principal.

The program gets started and one by one the children came and gave their speech. Their speech was not that long, they are just 6 years old. Everyone were adorable and cute. Both me and Jason are waiting for Ella to listen her speech. Next one is Ella. We both are excited. Jason is literally jumping in his seat.

She stands in front of microphone. "Good morning everyone, my name is Ella Knight. Today I am here to give a speech on topic My mother", my eyes widened. She looks at me and smiles. Jason holds my hand tightly.

She takes a long breath. "My mother is my first friend. She inspires me to be a better person. She wakes up every morning before dawn and prepares breakfast and my tiffin box. She is a doctor. She works till late night, to make the lives of everyone around her better.

When I fall sick she stays up all night to look after me and be there by my side and the next morning she goes about her daily routine. She takes care of my family and also her patients at the hospital. She taught me to be kind and respectful. My mother is the best mother in the world. I love you Mama."

I didn't realize that I'm crying. Tears runs down from my cheek. She----She called me Mama. She gave a speech about me. She waves her hand at me and gives me a flying kiss. Jason claps and whistles. "She is my daughter", he kept saying this to everyone beside him. Jason wipes my tears.

"You heard that right? She called me-----"Yes baby, she called you Mama. I'm so happy today", Jason hugs me. I still can't believe that she called me Mama. After everyone's speech was over, Ella runs towards me. Seeing her I couldn't stop my tears again.

I lift her up in my arms, "Mama, don't cry", she wipes my tears. I laugh. This feeling is new and it feels so good. "You did so good today.""I love you Mama", she kissed my cheek. "I love too Ella."

Jason wraps his arms around us from behind and kissed our forehead. "Let's go somewhere to eat, I'm starving.""I want ice cream", Ella said. "Of course, but only when you finish your food.""Okay Mama", she nods and runs towards the car and Jason runs behind her scolding her.

I run behind them. "Hey, I am joining too.""Kira! You too? What I've said about running?", Jason starts scolding me too.

"Mister, you can't talk to me like that. Better keep that attitude to yourself", I said. We sit at the backseat of the car. "Papa got scolding from Mama",

Ella teases Jason making me laugh. Jason tickles both of us. They both are my world. We are a happy family.

———————————

Few months later

"What's up with you? You are yawning like a lot today?", April reminds me and I yawn again. "You know, you should be preparing for your wedding, which is in two days?", she gives me a glass of water.

"I don't know. From two-three days I'm feeling dizzy inspite of sleeping for good hours daily. I'm tired. Today while eating breakfast I felt like vomiting. The wedding is in two days and I missed my period. I think I ate something wrong", I said and yawn again.

"No, I think-----", April didn't complete it, but it clicked me. We both instantly looked at each other. April smirked at me. "No it's not", I shake my head in denial. "Of course it is bitch. We need to test", April grabs my hand and drags me with her.

"Where are you taking me?.""Kira we work in a fucking hospital. We need to check up. You know that you are pregnant too, so keep quite."

"Congratulations bitch. Now I'm aunt of two kids", April is jumping around everywhere. I'm pregnant. We are going to have one more member in our family. I touch my belly. Ella is going to have a sister or brother. Jason and I are going to have a second child.

I told April to not tell this to anyone until I give this news to Jason. Everybody is busy doing arrangements for the wedding. April, Arlo, Julius, Liam, Aliana and Kelly, they all are staying with us till our wedding.

Jason is busy with the boys talking with them. We all had dinner together. After dinner I head upstairs to our room, while others are enjoying their time. Ella is sleeping in her bedroom. I go to the balcony to get some fresh air. A pair of arms wrapped around me and I know it is Jason.

"Finally, we are alone", he kissed my shoulder blade. I turn to face him. "I want to tell you something.""What?.""I'm pregnant. I found out today", his eyes widened.

"We---We are going to have another Angel?", I laugh and nod at him. "It can be a boy too.""I know. I love you so much", he lifts me up in his arms.

"You make me so happy baby", he kisses me all over my face. "Thank you so much", he doesn't stop kissing me. "Ella is going to be a big sister. I will tell her-------", he was all ready to go to Ella and wake her up now.

"No Laszlo. She is sleeping right now. You can tell her tomorrow", I kiss him"Okay. I will tell this to everyone now", he runs down to tell everyone and I laugh at his actions.

I go down. Everyone is hugging and congratulating Jason. "We want a double party now", Aaliana shouts and everyone cheers with her.

Wedding Day

"You look stunning darling, absolutely beautiful", Julia compliments me as I am ready in my wedding dress. "Thanks mom", she kisses my cheekI've started calling her mom, she has given me all the love and she cares for me a lot. "Let's go."

Everyone are patiently waiting for us. I walk down the aisle. Jason as always he is looking handsome in black tuxedo. He wipes his tears away and takes my hand. We both stand in front of priest.

"Welcome family and friends. We are gathered here today to witness and celebrate the marriage of-----------", the officiant continues, not once did I and Jason broke our eye contact.

"You have your vows ready?", the priest asked. "I will say", I prepared my vows."Jason Laszlo Knight. I can't describe how fortunate I am to have you in my life. We both had our ups and downs, but we went through all that obstacles together. I'm glad you didn't gave up on me. You gave me so much to cherish in our life. We have Ella and now we are going to have one more member in our family.

Jason, your name itself means 'healer'. You healed me baby. I can't imagine my life without you. I love you Laszlo", his eyes were moist.

"I love you too Kira", we both smile at each other. We exchange our rings. We said 'I do', when the priest asked us as lawful husband and wife.

"You may kiss the bride", the priest announced. Finally. Jason leaned down and kissed me and I wrap my arms around him. Everyone cheered for us. We pull away. Ella is also cheering and waving at us. Jason pecks my lips again. "I love you Mr. Knight.""I love you too Mrs. Knight."

EPILOGUE

JASON

Kira is five months pregnant now. I decided that I should work from home. I only go out for important meeting but the rest of my work, I do it from home.

"I'm gonna miss my work", she says as she enters our bedroom. She is taking a break till the delivery. When I told her that she should take a break, first she got angry at me and didn't talked to me for whole day. But later I made her understand that she and the baby, both need a lot of rest.

"Finally", I wrap my arms around her waist and kissed her lips. "I need to pick up Ella from school", I keep our lips touching against each other. "Hmm...When you come home I want some pasta. Your's are the best", I laugh and kiss her cheek.

Meanwhile I go to Ella's school to pick her up. She is really good with her studies and also in sports. She already made many friends in her school. I take her hand in mine, "Let's go Angel. We need to buy some ice cream for your Mama"."I want chocolate.""Of course Ella."

I bring three tubs of chocolate ice cream. Kira cravings always changes and also her mood swings. One late night she wanted chicken wings, other night she wanted Chinese food and yesterday she wanted chocolate ice cream. We only had vanilla flavour at home and she literally cried for that.

I love to do anything for her. Even if it means to handle her mood swings. She looks really scary when she is angry at me. We reach home. Ella straight goes to Kira, who is in kitchen.

"Mama, we brought ice cream for you.""Thank you Angel", Kira kissed her cheek. "Go freshen up okay?", Angel giggles and nods at her.

I give Kira ice cream and she keeps in fridge. I chop some vegetables for pasta. "Jason, where is my donut?." Fuck me. "Umm...I ate it today", I face her, she already looks like she is going to cry.

"Baby you said you didn't wanted to eat it, and only one donut was left.""I wanted to eat it today. Fuck you Jason", she runs crying upstairs. "Don't run baby. You will hurt yourself." Fuck, why did I eat it.

I wanted to go to her but she will not listen to me and she is hungry. So, I try to cook fast. I also prepare her favourite sandwich with some juice. I ask one of the maids to cook Ella's favorite dish for her, while I give this to Kira.

Kira covered herself in the blanket. I tried to remove it, but she held it tightly. "Look I cooked pasta and also your favorite sandwich with some juice", she immediately removed the covers and I laugh at her, as she starts eating her food.

"I'm still mad at you"."I will tell someone to bring you dozens of donuts, okay?", she nods and I kiss her cheek and her baby bump. "My little pea is troubling you a lot, huh?", I keep my hand on her belly.

"Hmm... I want our little pea to come out as soon as possible", she keeps her hand on mine. "You're right, because we are going to have more little peas", I try to mess with her and she stops eating and looks shocked.

"How many exactly do you want?.""I don't know, maybe three or four more", I try hard to not laugh at her. "Yeah not going to happen. Why don't you try being pregnant or find another woman", she rubs her belly.

"No baby, you forever", I kiss her forehead. "Jason, will you bring some more pasta for me", she innocently smiles at me. "Sure baby."